URBAN goddess

You are a goddess!!
Believe in you :)
S Hayes
06/22/12

by Sonia Hayes

NUA Multimedia
4611 Hardscrabble Road
Suite 109, PMB 309
Columbia, SC 29229

Cover design by Diane Florence
Author Portrait by Ron MacDonald

ISBN: 978-0-9777573-1-2

LCCN: 2006911323

In loving memory of my father,

Kenneth Kirkland

This book is dedicated to

The young ladies of the Delta Academy, YWCA and the Girl Scouts of America programs across the country. Many of whom I have had the pleasure of meeting during the *Ms. Thang* book discussions. You make my journey worthwhile. Thank you for your support.

Acknowledgments

Super Trooper, thank you for all the ways you have contributed to my development, both professionally and personally. To the flyest cheerleader I know, Sonia P., thank you for being my reader and number one fan. My darlings, Sasha and Savanna, thank you for allowing me to devote time to this project. Khari and Kirah, thank you for being there when I needed help with the little ones. AEP3, thank you so much for the edits. Barbara P., thank you for helping promote and sell *Ms. Thang*. Trish M., your honest critiques were instrumental in the evolution of *Urban Goddess*, thank you. Kyra M., thank you for being my first reader, even though you sneaked a peek. Lucy B.A.W.W., you have always been there for me since UWM, much love. Elgin, thanks for being a friend. To my editor, Ann Fisher, thank you. Last but not least, thanks to all the fans for keeping the pressure on me to complete the sequel. I did it for you, enjoy!

URBAN *goddess*

Chapter 1

Shaniqua leaned her petite frame against the concrete pillar with one hand on her cocked hip in the noisy commons area of Miller Grove High School. Students were yelling to get one another's attention, girls displaying their high-pitched giggles and a few football jocks tussling like eight year olds with each other. Like most students during the first few days of school, Shaniqua looked crisp and happy until monotony set in. Dressed in a black mini-skirt, orange V-neck top, and four-inch pumps, she watched the other students hugging one another, and like her, jockeying for position to be in the "in" crowd.

Shaniqua arrived early that morning, determined to get her posse a space. It was a ritual for the cool upperclassmen to hang out in the commons area every morning before school. Nothing would remove her from her post, not even if she spotted Cherise, the cockroach and the creepy-crawlers. Shaniqua shifted her weight to one leg and let her freshly done micro braids rest across her narrow back. She busied herself by examining her new acrylic nails tips, hoping her little pink pimple remained unnoticeable—that it wasn't bursting through the thick cover-up used to conceal it. Her skin was bright, like she was not entirely black, and the fact that her hair was very bushy when it wasn't braided, suggested a slight strain of another race's blood. Suddenly, a hard arm thump prompted her to turn around.

"Ouch!" Shaniqua said, examining the red mark on her arm. She spun around and looked down through hazel-colored contacts. "Tasha, stand up and quit playing!"

Natasha burst into laughter. "Ahh, I had you going!"

"No, you didn't! What's up, girl?" Shaniqua held her arms open. "Show me some love, show me some love."

"I just saw you last week." Natasha rolled her eyes heavenward and stooped over to give her a hug.

"Get off me now, you're messing up my new gear," Shaniqua said, playfully brushing her skirt. "Where's Brittany?"

"I don't know." Natasha scanned the area. "Oh, here she comes now."

Brittany sashayed over and struck a sassy pose with one hand on her cocked hip, "Holla at a goddess!"

Shaniqua twirled around and struck a sassy pose, too. "Oh, no, I'm the goddess!"

All three girls burst into laughter.

Brittany looked Shaniqua over and then leaned in for a hug. "Hey, hot Momma!"

Shaniqua wiggled her shapely, petite hips, her oversized gold doorknocker earrings danced along. "Y'all, we're jamming jade juniors! Heyyyy!"

Brittany puckered her eyebrows, "What is a jade?"

"Hell if I know, but it sound good," Shaniqua said, swinging her braids out of her face, letting them cascade like strings of yarn.

Brittany flashed her famous smirk. The one that turned her plump lips into two tight lines. "It sounds good."

Shaniqua positioned her hands around her tiny waistline. "Welcome back, Ms. Perfect," she said, and then looked to Natasha. "So what's up for this school year? We got to get crunk! We're upperclassmen, you know!"

Brittany swept hair behind her ear and then looked at Natasha, clad in black Capri's and a fitted coral-colored top. "Uh-oohhh, look at Ms. Thang, tomboy turned supermodel. She has on makeup and her eyebrows are arched!"

Shaniqua cupped Natasha's chin. "Let me see."

Natasha stepped back. "Dang, you don't have to put your hands all in my face."

"Oh, no, this is the *real* goddess right here. You can't even touch her!" Shaniqua said. "How does Stephen like your new look, huh, Mrs. Perry?"

Brittany and Shaniqua slapped high-fives and cracked up laughing.

Natasha looked down at her watch. "I'm out, see you guys at lunch." Her long legs took extensive strides to get away from them quickly, forgetting everything the modeling school had taught her about walking.

Brittany batted her eyelashes like butterfly wings. "See ya afta wol, Mrs. Perry," she said in an exaggerated Southern drawl.

Brittany and Shaniqua lingered around to catch up since they were not the type of friends who called one another over the summer break. They connected mostly through Natasha.

Shaniqua shifted her weight to one leg, studying Brittany. "So how was your summer, girl? I see you've been eating good."

Brittany's smile turned into a frown.

Shaniqua tossed her head back in a laugh and then placed her bony arm around Brittany's shoulders. "I'm just kidding, dang. Chill!"

"Well, at least my legs don't look like two stilts!" Brittany said, still refusing to smile. Brittany knew Shaniqua was right. She had regained the weight that she lost after the car accident last year. She now tipped the scales at 155 lbs. and stood 5'5". Brittany searched around for something to say, but no words came, so she offered a sly grin. "So, how are you feeling since the . . . you know? I mean, do you get your periods regularly again?"

"What?"

"Oh, girl, look over there," Brittany said, pointing across the hallway.

"Ugh, Jordan Kelley! Girl please, I ain't thinking about his cockroach-looking self or his girlfriend, Mrs. Cockroach."

"They broke up," Brittany whispered. "I'm not one to

gossip, so you haven't heard this from me, but I heard he gave her a STD. Shhh, here she comes, pretend like you don't see her."

Shaniqua's face tightened as she studied the designs in the beige terrazzo floor. She wondered if it was herpes, the same gift Jordan had given her. Most days Shaniqua was fine, but occasionally she had days when it was uncomfortable for her to sit.

Silence seized the moment while Cherise and her two sidekicks passed by. "Slut! I wonder who she's going to get pregnant for this year?" one of the girls said. They cackled like hyenas and kept walking.

Their words pierced Shaniqua's chest like a machete, threatening tears.

Brittany draped her arm around Shaniqua's shoulders. "Just ignore them. That was last year and this is a new year. Cherise is just jealous of you because of Jordan."

Shaniqua nodded, "That's why she's a senior with a face that still looks like a Nestlé Crunch candy bar."

"Girl, you're crazy, see you at lunch."

Shaniqua headed to homeroom wondering if Jordan Kelley would be in there again this year or if he had failed the tenth grade for a second time. She really hoped the latter; that way she wouldn't have to see him every morning. Shaniqua skimmed past Mrs. Roberson's desk.

"Uh, Ms. Williams, come back here," Mrs. Roberson said.

Shaniqua stood to the side of Mrs. Roberson's desk, waiting for her to finish filing papers away in a desk drawer. Shaniqua watched Hailey Heinecke bouncing around the classroom as if she were campaigning for an election of some sort, giggling and smiling. Everything in life wasn't that frickin' amusing. Maybe for girls like Hailey it was—she had both parents and money. Shaniqua had neither parents nor money.

Jordan's voice could be heard as he approached the classroom, laughing with his buddies, Rick and James. All three boys entered the room, their pants sagging down to their knees. None of them seemed to have grown over the summer. No wonder Jordan pretended to be tougher than he was; he suffered from the "little man" complex. Though Shaniqua couldn't really talk—she hadn't grown much over the summer either, she was still 5'2".

Shaniqua kept her attention toward the front of the class, just as she had the second semester of their sophomore year. Ignoring Jordan would be easy. After all the crap he had put her through, she really didn't care if his lungs ever took in air again. *Little worthless weasel.*

Mrs. Roberson stood up, wobbled over to the other side of her desk, her thunder thighs jiggling. "Ms. Williams, put your things down and do the fingertip test."

Shaniqua rolled her eyes. Mrs. Roberson was forever hassling her about her gear. She was sure Mrs. Roberson was just jealous because she couldn't fit her oversized turkey legs in a skirt. "Mrs. Roberson, my skirt ain't too short."

"Place your hands at your side, Ms. Williams. You know the routine. If your fingertips reach past your skirt, you need to change clothes."

Shaniqua slapped her arms against both sides to perform the test.

Mrs. Roberson nodded. "Sorry, Ms. Williams, you know the rule."

"My skirt ain't too short, I have long arms."

The class burst into laughter. Someone whistled. Shaniqua swore she heard Jordan's voice, "Damn, she's finer than last year."

"Hell yeah!" Rick added.

"Shaniqua, keep pleading your case, and I'll be happy to discuss this with you after school in detention, your choice," Mrs. Roberson said, then took her seat in the too small chair, letting the extra flesh trail off the sides. She stared out at the class. "Well, it's certainly nice to see you all again, welcome back. I trust you all had a wonderful summer break."

A few cheers and moans resonated around the room.

Shaniqua slumped in her chair. There was no way that Granny was going to come to school just to bring her a change of clothes. First off, Granny didn't own a car. Secondly, Shaniqua had secretly borrowed the outfit from her cousin, Renee. She had to get Mrs. Roberson not to send her home.

"I need a volunteer, please," Mrs. Roberson said.

Hailey's hand shot up in the air like a rocket. "I'll help," her high-pitched voice chimed, making Shaniqua want to cram her ears with cotton.

Mrs. Roberson handed Hailey a stack of papers to pass out. Not much had changed over the summer. Mrs. Roberson's inverted ski slope of a chin was still smooth as ever, and jiggled when she talked. Hailey was still the teacher's pet, thin as a toothpick, and still masquerading as a blonde, evident by her dark eyebrows and aqua-blue contacts.

The morning announcements came on, lighting up the wall-mounted television screen. Principal Anderson carried on about nothing, until Shaniqua heard cheerleading tryouts. Her ears perked up like a pet poodle's, but it was too late; she missed the information. She could always ask Hailey, the professional cheerleader, since she'd been on the varsity squad since freshman year.

Without turning her head to confirm her suspicion, Shaniqua knew that Jordan, Rick, and James were talking about her. They kept looking two rows over as if they were trying to get her attention. Shaniqua knew she looked cute that morning. She had stayed away from chocolate and soda all summer, just to make sure her face would be clear by the time school started.

The bell sounded, ending homeroom and sending students into the noisy, chaotic hallways. Shaniqua stalled in her seat until Jordan and his crew left. She didn't want to hear anything they had to say. Just because it was a new school year didn't mean that they could start out fresh, as if nothing ever happened.

"Ah, Ms. Williams," Mrs. Roberson said, motioning for Shaniqua to come up to her desk.

Shaniqua gathered her belongings and made her way up front. She hoped it wouldn't take long; she needed to talk with Hailey. "Yes, ma'am?"

"Because it's the first day of school, I'm going to excuse you for being inappropriately dressed today. However, if you decide to take it upon yourself to come to school dressed inappropriately tomorrow, you will be sent home. Do we have an understanding?"

"Yes, ma'am," Shaniqua said, watching Hailey leave the classroom. "Thank you." Quickly, she caught up to her. "Hey, Hailey, when are cheerleading tryouts being held?"

Hailey looked Shaniqua over and then offered a fake smile that coincided perfectly with her fake bleach blonde hair. "Next week."

"What do I need to do?"

Hailey's smile vanished. "There's an information sheet posted on the activity board in the front lobby," she said, then pushed past Shaniqua.

"Thanks, little witch," Shaniqua muttered to herself on the way to her first period class, when suddenly out of nowhere, she heard, "Yo Shorty Red?" It sounded like Jordan Kelley's voice. There was no way he would be speaking to her after all that had happened between them. She turned around slowly. Jordan was walking towards her. Her heart raced. He didn't sound as if he was going to try to fight her again but she wasn't sure. She scanned the area for help. Maybe Natasha's brother, Nate would jump in again and knock Jordan out like he did last year.

"Shorty Red?" He said again.

Shaniqua stood frozen. She couldn't believe that Jordan had the audacity to speak to her. Had he lost his freakin' mind? What could he possibly have to say to her? All the disgust that she felt toward him poured out of her facial expression.

"Dang girl, why you mean muggin' me?"

"We ain't got nothing to talk about."

Jordan's voice softened as he inched closer to her, "I got something I've been meaning to say to you since last year."

Shaniqua shifted her weight to one leg and stared at him blankly.

Jordan shoved his hands in his two front pockets and ogled the floor. "I know this is going to come as a surprise, but uh, I'm sorry."

"For?"

He looked around to see if anyone was watching. The hallway had thinned out. Most kids were already in class. "About last year."

Shaniqua refrained from speaking and continued staring at him, searching his eyes for truth. Though, they had deceived her once before. Granny always said eyes were the windows to a person's soul.

"I want to make it up to you."

"Make it up to me? How?"

Jordan whipped out a thick wad of twenties from his front pants pocket and counted out two hundred dollars. "Here."

Shaniqua's eyes bucked. "Where you get that money from?"

He popped his collar. "I'm a h-u-s-t-l-e-r, hustla."

She giggled.

Jordan grabbed Shaniqua's hand and placed the money in her palm. "I got plenty mo' where that came from," he said, then offered a mischievous grin.

The money felt good in her hand. Her mind raced to all the things she could do with it. She could buy some new school clothes of her own. That way she wouldn't have to wear her cousin Nee Nee's clothes. Maybe even a little trac phone. But something about the way Jordan was smiling made her uncomfortable. Shaniqua shoved the money back at him. "That's alright."

"Get at me if you change yo' mind."

Shaniqua nodded.

"So what's up, can I call you?"

"I don't know about all that."

"Well, when you do know, holla at me," he said grinning.

Shaniqua hated to admit it, but Jordan looked cute. The diamond studs in his earlobes were twice the size as the ones he rocked last year and sparkled along with his shiny platinum grill. His hair was neatly braided in a zigzag pattern. He looked as though he had spent a lot of time in the sun over the summer because his complexion was about three shades darker than normal, resembling dark chocolate. Just maybe she and Jordan could change things between them, she thought making her way to class late.

Chapter 2

Brittany waved to a few students as she made her way into the noisy girls' bathroom. She was still riding high from the popularity that last year's car accident had won her. Judging from all the smiling faces that greeted hers, she knew that kids still remembered her. She wondered if the other students still thought about Jared. Occasionally, Brittany thought about him, mostly whenever she was riding in the car with her brother, Kevin. Like Jared, Kevin loved to race his Mustang. Brittany sometimes wondered how Jared's parents were doing, but she just couldn't bring herself to call. It would probably stir up too many painful memories for them. There was no way she could bring Jared back, no way to ease the tragic loss his parents had suffered. It was best to leave well enough alone.

Standing over the bathroom sink, Brittany slid her sparkling diamond studs out of her earlobes, tucked them safely in their black velvet box and snapped it shut with authority. She dug around in her purse for her forbidden large hoop earrings, and put them on. She patted her forehead with facial blotting tissue to absorb the excess oil and reduce the shine. Next, she tousled her hair so that her long layers looked like they were unsettled. She applied a light layer of mascara, dabbed on pink-tinted lip-gloss, then flashed a quick smile in the mirror for reassurance.

Brittany was a beautiful girl by anyone's standards. She had an attractive smile that stretched wide to reveal perfectly straight teeth. She had soft doe eyes and chubby cheeks, as if she still carried baby fat except she wasn't a baby anymore. Her skin was like a smooth cocoa bean. Brittany dug around the bottom of her purse for her spare bottle of perfume–a luxury she hadn't done without since the seventh grade. Her mom always said, "A well-bred young lady always smells of sophisticated scents." Like her mom, Brittany wore the pricey stuff, not the cheap cologne that tried to pass as perfume.

Brittany plunked into her seat in Chemistry class, keeping her head down as the teacher began speaking. There was nothing new to look at—the same boring students—so she doodled on her notebook: "Brittany Ann Brown, the flyest cheerleader of them all," in pink gel ink. If she had her way, she would have never taken honors courses. The fun, cool kids were never in her classes. No one ever mouthed off to the teachers and went to ISD. Sometimes, Brittany thought of doing something just to get out of class, but the repercussions were too severe. Her dad wouldn't hesitate to come up to the school and show out. Brittany squirmed in her seat, listening to Mr. Ragsdale go over the course syllabus. She was getting pretty tired of being "Ms. Perfect" as her friends always referred to her. Daily, her parents sucked the life right out of her with their strict rules, no make-up, no dating, no boys calling the house, must get straight A's, blah blah blah. It was ridiculous that her outfits had to win the approval of her mother every morning. Her own bedroom wasn't even decorated the way she wanted. It was her mother's idea, along with the professional interior designer, to create a soft, frilly, romantic look for her daughter. She hated that room. She needed to find some way to escape from her parents, from their prison, the Brown Compound. Cheerleading would be the route she decided as she continued doodling.

When the lunch bell rang students rushed out into the halls like cattle in a stampede. Shaniqua hurriedly shoved her books into her locker and headed downstairs. The cafeteria was loud with the usual sounds of plastic trays slamming against the tables, metal forks and spoons clinking while the students seemed to be speaking at an unusually high decibel level. The cafeteria had the same mustard colored walls, the same snag-a-tooth head cook and the same shabby lunch tables. The only interesting thing would be seeing who would get the popular tables near the front. Some seniors had already claimed the best ones. Shaniqua searched for another spot halfway back, but students were claiming tables quicker than poor people cashed lottery tickets. Shaniqua kept walking, passing the jocks, the cool Asians, and the preps until she reached an empty table sandwiched between some freshmen geeks and a group of girls who looked like they didn't eat at all. The table was even further back than the one they had last year.

Shaniqua grabbed her lunch, sat down, and waited for Natasha and Brittany. The August heat made eating outside impossible. She studied her friends as they emerged from the long lunch line. They really hadn't changed much either this year. Though Brittany had picked up weight again, she looked cute in her long pink crepe skirt and matching Fendi sunglasses perched atop her head. Natasha hadn't grown any more—she was holding steady at 5'10". Something was different about Natasha, though. Shaniqua couldn't quite put her finger on it. Maybe that modeling class was really helping.

"Alright, gossip time," Shaniqua said. "Who got the fine boys in their classes this year?"

Brittany rolled her eyes, "Puh-leeze, we're talking about Miller Grove High, there aren't any fine boys here."

Natasha nodded in agreement with Brittany.

Shaniqua pursed her lips. "Tasha, you really need to

quit frontin'. Isn't Stephen Perry in your classes?"

"Maybe in Art II. Anyway, I keep telling y'all we're just friends."

Brittany stuffed French fries in her mouth. "And we keep telling you that nobody creates a huge oil painting of just some girl that they don't like and then gives it to her for a Christmas present. Duh!" Brittany and Shaniqua slapped high-fives.

"Y'all will never guess who spoke to me today," Shaniqua said.

Brittany and Natasha looked at each other and said in unison, "Who?"

"Jordan Kelley."

Brittany nearly gagged on her food. "What! I know you played him to the left."

"What did he say?" Natasha asked.

"He apologized."

"Apologized? Oh hell no!" Brittany shouted.

Natasha turned to Brittany. "Be quiet Brit, let Shaniqua speak."

"I was just as shocked as y'all, trust me."

"So what did you say to him?" Natasha asked.

"I said, okay."

"Okay?" Brittany frowned. "You should've spit in his face!"

"He seemed pretty sincere. Oh-my-God, y'all he was looking too cute."

Brittany's wide eyes narrowed to two slanted lines. "What! Shaniqua, you really need to check yourself. All I have to say is, you're beyond stupid if you get involved with him again."

"Yeah, Shaniqua, Brittany's right. That little creep needn't look your way."

"I ain't thinking about him."

Brittany pursed her lips. "Yeah, right, Shaniqua. We'll see."

Shaniqua took a sip of milk. "Guess what, y'all? I'm thinking of going out for cheerleading,"

Brittany offered a sour smile. "You?"

"Yes, me. Why not?"

"No reason, I'm just surprised, that's all." Brittany smiled; her dimples were cutting so deeply they looked like slits in her face. "I'm trying out, too."

"Cool, let's try out together. You game, Tasha?" Shaniqua said.

"Nope, I'll be playing varsity basketball?"

"So, Ms. Thang, the prissy model, isn't going to give up basketball?" Brittany turned back to Shaniqua. "You want to come over Saturday and let my mom help us get ready for tryouts? She used to cheer for East Lithonia High back in the day, way back in the day."

They all laughed.

"Cool, I'll see if my cousin, Nee Nee, can drop me off."

"We can take you home afterwards. Tasha, you want to come and hang out, too?" Brittany asked.

"Can't. I've got my first modeling session in the advanced class."

"Wow, you're really serious with this thing, huh?" Shaniqua said.

Natasha nodded. "We're having our fashion show at Lenox."

Shaniqua bit off the tip of her French-fry. "Dang, Tasha, you're going to have to model clothes in front of all those people at the mall? Uh-uh, no way, you can have that."

Brittany slid her sunglasses down from her head and onto her face, a cheesy grin spread from cheek to cheek. "Ladies, you know I'm turning sixteen in a few weeks. And since I didn't get to celebrate my birthday last year because I was in the hospital, my parents are throwing me a super sweet-sixteen soiree," she said, batting her eyelashes.

"What is a soiree?" Shaniqua mocked snooty-like.

Brittany rolled her eyes. "Shaniqua, it's just another word for party. Get some class!"

"You get some!"

"Anyway, my parents are going all out. My mom hired a party planner and ordered the fabric for my dress from Paris. Il est trés, trés belle. It's going to be in a ballroom at the historic Georgian Terrace Hotel on Peachtree Street. I'm so excited."

"Wow! That's really nice of your folks," Natasha said. "Shoot, all my parents did for my sweet sixteen was take me to the Cheesecake Factory and gave me cash."

Brittany bit into her hamburger, then playfully inspected her fingernails while she swallowed. "So, I guess I'll let y'all come. I'll have to check my guest list first."

URBAN GODDESS

Natasha headed to her seventh period class conscious of her strides, not wanting to fall back into the "Jolly Green Giant" mode of walking. He was history and she never wanted to think of herself as his twin again. Her height was something to be proud of, she constantly reminded herself. No longer would she slouch just to appear a few inches shorter. Natasha had worked hard over the summer to erase those thoughts from her consciousness.

She entered art class. Sculptures, charcoal drawings, oil portraits, water-colored abstracts decorated the room. Natasha took the same seat near the front that she had last year, just in case Stephen Perry was in her class again. She would have preferred to sit in the back, but if Stephen walked in, she wouldn't want him to think that she didn't want to sit by him. They had talked on the phone a couple of times over the summer, but she hadn't seen him since the last day of school.

Stephen appeared in the doorway, dressed casually in cargo pants and a brightly colored, plaid button-down shirt. Natasha's heart beat faster. He looked good. Different. She studied him. His hair had grown and was now twisted. His hazel eyes gleamed with excitement, while his lips curled into a soft smile. He seemed much cooler, hotter.

Natasha tried hard not to blush, "Hey!"

Stephen stretched out his arms for a hug. "What's up, Tasha!"

She knew she was smiling hard and unsophisticatedly, just like the green man on the vegetable can. Natasha silently prayed that the other students weren't watching her make a fool of herself. *Ho, ho, ho, Green Giant*!

Stephen placed his books on the floor and sat beside her just as he did last year. "So, did you do anything interesting over the summer?"

Natasha smiled and shook her head. "Not really, how about you?"

"My dad opened a sub-sandwich business, so I worked there. I did another oil painting.

"Really, of what or who?"

The teacher cleared his throat in a lame attempt to get the students' attention. "Good afternoon, everyone. My name is Mr. Arnold," he said, scanning the room, his wire-rimmed eyeglasses sitting at the tip of his nose. "Some of you are new students, but it looks like I had many of you in previous classes. So, welcome back."

Natasha was glad that she had Mr. Arnold again. He was cool in a sort of '60s hippie-type way. He continued talking about the necessary supplies and objectives for the course.

When class ended, she tried to employ what she had learned in her modeling class. With the beginner's class instructor Isabella's thick Italian accent echoing in her head, Natasha made her way to the door, "Stand up straight, chest out, stomach in, walk lifting your thighs. You can tell a lot about a person just from the way they walk."

Stephen caught up to her. "Tasha, wait up, I'll walk with you."

Natasha turned, and shifted her weight onto one leg, trying to act as if it wasn't a big deal, her long arms dangling loosely at her sides—she hadn't figured out what to do with them yet. Stephen's cologne infused her nostrils with a clean, crisp mix of iris and musk.

"So, what do you like to do on the weekends, besides play basketball with your brothers?" Stephen asked.

Natasha focused on his Adam's apple, which seemed to have grown since last year. "Nothing really. I'm starting my modeling classes on Saturday."

"Oh, I thought you did that last year."

"I did. I'm taking the advanced class now."

"So you're getting pretty serious with this, huh?"

Natasha studied the large tile squares in the floor. "Yeah, I really like it."

"Well, you look awesome."

Natasha offered a tight-lipped grin, and then slid her shoulder-length hair behind her ear as if it were in the way. She had seen Brittany do it a million times. "Thanks."

"So you want to catch a movie or something on the weekend? I got my license this summer, so my dad lets me take the car whenever I want."

"I got mine, too. Yes, that'd be cool."

"I'll call you Saturday afternoon," Stephen said and hurried down the corridor.

Natasha wanted to die a quick hard death, right there on the well-polished floor. They would say she died a happy student. Someone had finally asked her out. Not just anyone, but Stephen Perry. She could finally admit it now, if not to her friends then to herself, she had had a serious crush on him in ninth grade. But they never spoke to one another, not even 'hi.' Natasha bet he didn't even know their lockers were down the hall from one another. Then last year, they became good platonic friends. They shared a passion for art. Every time Natasha looked at the portrait that Stephen painted for her as a Christmas gift, it reminded her of the special bond that they shared. Now it was official. Stephen had made his interest in her known. No more platonic get-togethers. Stephen had asked her specifically to go out on a date.

She wanted to share the news with her girls, but the more she thought about it, maybe it was just another platonic get-together. It's not like he said, "Oh Tasha, I've been digging on you since last year, and just never had the courage to push up." Natasha decided she would share the news with them, but not in the way of a date. It wasn't a date. It was a get-together, she reminded herself.

Chapter 3

Early Saturday morning, the smell of bacon penetrated Shaniqua's bedroom prompting her to throw the old shaggy rug-like blanket off her. The blanket was probably white many years ago, but now it was the same dull eggshell color as the walls. Her bedroom had very little color in it. The only color came from the array of posters plastered around her room. A Lil' Kim poster hung above her bed so she could easily look up and see it first thing in the morning for inspiration.

Shaniqua rambled through her drawers looking for something to wear to cheerleading practice. She decided on a white wife beater and black short shorts. She showered and then put in her contacts lenses. Seldom did a day pass that she didn't wear them. She gathered her braids into a high ponytail, slid her favorite large hoop earrings through her earlobes and then secured her gold-plated name necklace around her neck. Lastly, she dabbed on peach tinted lip-gloss, and made her way downstairs into the kitchen where Granny was standing over the stove flipping homemade flapjacks. Granny was a big boned woman in striking contrast to her petite granddaughter. Her skin was deep brown against her salt and pepper hair. Shaniqua leaned over and planted a soft kiss on her grandmother's cheek. "Morning, Granny."

"Morning, baby, go 'head and fix yo' plate why the food's hot."

Shaniqua was loading her plate with pecan pancakes, cheese eggs, grits and crispy bacon when she heard a car pull up in front of the house. Glancing at the watermelon clock above the sink, Shaniqua realized that it was much too early for Nee Nee to pick her up to take her to Brittany's house.

"Alright, now, you take care." Shaniqua thought she heard her mother's voice. Her eyes quickly stole to Granny who was busy washing dishes. Suddenly, Shaniqua leaped up from the kitchen table, ran to the living room window and peeked out Granny style ducking behind the heavy brown curtain.

Karen was extremely skinny, gaunt-looking. Shaniqua could just hear the kids making fun of her. "Yo' momma so skinny she can hoola hoop with a Cheerio!" Karen's hair was wild and bushy like Don King's except it was black.

Shaniqua leaped up the stairs, taking three at a time. The doorbell buzzed. Shaniqua plopped down on her bed and pretended to read the upside down magazine. *What kind of mother showed up every few years?* The bell sounded again. This time she heard Granny saying, "Chil'ren ain't fit for nothin' these days." Shaniqua could tell by the sudden creaking in the floor that Granny was walking to the door.

"Yes," Granny said, swinging open the door. "My, my, look what the cat done drug in!"

"Mornin', Momma!" Karen said. Her eyes were red, so red they looked permanent as if she had been born that way. Karen wrapped her arms around Granny's thick waistline.

Granny returned the hug with a one-arm squeeze around Karen's bony shoulders. "Girl, what's the matter with you? You withering away to nothin'." Granny stepped back to examine her daughter's rail-thin frame. "Every time I see you, you get smaller and smaller. You all right?"

"Yes, ma'am." Karen said.

"Why you walkin' around looking like you hungry then?"

Karen glanced around, "Where's my baby?"

"Shaniqua!" Granny yelled up the stairs.

After a couple of minutes, Granny tried again. "Shaniqua, you hear me callin' you? Git down here!"

Shaniqua threw the old Cosmo Girl magazine on the floor, then trampled on it. None of the articles ever pertained to girls of color. She wished she could step on Karen the same way. Why did her mother even bother coming back? No good ever came out of her returning home. Shaniqua took slow methodical steps downstairs. "Ma'am?'

"Yo' momma's here," Granny said.

"How's my beautiful baby girl?" Karen said, reaching to give Shaniqua a hug.

Shaniqua smelled her the moment they hugged.

Karen reeked of alcohol. To inhale it was like throwing a match into a puddle of gasoline, igniting pain in her body. Shaniqua had to remain calm, at least until she left again. Karen would be like a black cloud of smoke, graying, then dissipating. Shaniqua lifted her head. "Hey."

Karen's lips parted into a wide smile, revealing badly stained teeth. "You just as pretty as you wanna be!"

Shaniqua smirked. She had seen Brittany do it daily for three years. There was no way she was going to tell her mother that she was pretty, too. She couldn't see anything pretty about a woman who deserted her own child. People often told her that she bore a striking resemblance to Karen, except she was much lighter.

Granny hobbled down the hallway, "Y'all, let's go in the kitchen. Breakfast's gettin' cold."

Shaniqua clutched her hands over her stomach. "Granny, I don't feel good, I need to go lay down."

"Alright, baby. I'll put yo' plate in the oven."

Shaniqua took to her bed and planned to stay there until Karen left, which wouldn't be long. She rested her head on her flat, lumpy pillow and let her mind drift to the only good memories that she had of her mother. Shaniqua would run around searching for her colorful barrettes that were always scattered about Granny's house. Once she collected enough, she would hunt for the comb, brush and hair grease. It was a guessing game as to who was the last to use them, Granny, Karen, aunt Kathy or her cousin, Renee. Once Shaniqua gathered all the hair supplies, Karen would plant Shaniqua down on the floor right between her legs, while Karen sat on the sunken sofa. Her mother would first part and grease her scalp using the green Afro-sheen which smelled like sweet oil. Next, Shaniqua would plead with her mother to style her hair into one ponytail and leave it unbraided so it would look like she was wearing her hair down. Black girls only wore their hair down for special occasions like Easter Sunday and Christmas. Other than those occasions, it was one, two, three and the god-awful four-ponytail styles, with cute colorful barrettes clasped at the ends. And when Karen finished styling her hair, Shaniqua remembered her mom would ask for a kiss.

Shaniqua's eyes rested on her wrinkled Omarion poster, the same one she mistakenly crumpled up last year when she and Jordan started going out. It was time for Omarion to be replaced by Chris Brown. Shaniqua drifted off to sleep, knowing that when she awoke from her nap, Karen would be gone for a few more years.

Saturday morning, Natasha woke up at seven to prepare for her ten o'clock modeling class. In the first course, she had learned how to apply makeup for almost every occasion—the everyday look, glamour, photos, and television. Since her parents divorced when she was in the sixth grade, staying the night at her dad's house would not afford her the luxury of having a valid opinion.

It wasn't like her dad could say, "Princess, your blush is uneven" or "Smooth out your base." And she knew what her brothers would say if she asked Nate or Neil their opinions. "Ugh, take that garbage off! You don't need it!"

Natasha showered and studied her face in the close-up mirror. Her skin was smooth and the tone was an even, toasted almond shade. Natasha really didn't see why she needed to wear foundation, besides the fact that it was worn by all the other girls. And if she was the exception, the instructor might look at her as not being prepared. In her beginning class, the instructor kept stressing, "You may not always have a makeup artist on your assignment, so you need to learn how to look polished for all types of jobs. Come to class prepared like it's a modeling job."

After two hours of primping in the mirror, Natasha's dad dropped her off in front of the building in Buckhead. A large gray sign with red fancy lettering, displayed "Genesis Modeling and Finishing School." She stood to the side of the doorway, underneath the haze of heat dressed in a denim skirt and a red cotton top. It was only nine-thirty and already the heat index was over eighty degrees. A gentle breeze swept across her face as she studied the bumper-to-bumper traffic on Peachtree Street. No matter the time of day, Peachtree Street thrived with cars and pedestrians. The city of Atlanta grew around this one street. Natasha continued scanning the area looking for a familiar face, another girl to walk in with to keep the focus off her when she entered the school. When the humid September heat pressed beads of perspiration through the pores on her forehead and back, she had no choice but to enter the school alone or suffer the embarrassment of a sweat-stained shirt.

Her nerves rumbled in her stomach as she made her way through the double glass doors. Pictures of former students plastered the walls in the lobby and hallways. Some of the school's former students went on to become high-fashion models, and others pursued commercial work. Natasha stood erect on the burgundy carpet and checked her posture in the oversized mirror behind the receptionist's desk. Isabella's thick Italian accent echoed in her ears. "Natasha, if you want to become a model, you must stand like this, not like this," she said, slouching over to create a huge hump in her back. The whole class had burst into giggles, while Natasha had grinned to mask the hurt. Since that day, whenever she felt herself slouching, she straightened up, exceedingly so, that her mother asked her, "Why the inflated chest?"

Natasha surveyed the room and took a seat alongside the runway when she saw two girls from her previous class, Meagan and Emily. Natasha smiled at them as her self-doubt slowly crept in. All the girls were so beautiful—thin with pretty hair, straight white teeth, and stylish clothes. Natasha wondered if the other girls thought that she didn't belong. She always knew that she would never win anyone's beauty contest. And from the way the other girls looked at her, they knew it, too.

A woman with chiseled bone structure, sweeping blonde hair and legs that went on forever, stepped into the room and immediately took to the runway. The blue-eyed beauty glided down the catwalk, floating through the air. Her cream-colored wide-leg pants flared like a skirt. The cream bustier hugged her torso, creating ample cleavage. When the woman reached the end of the runway, she spun around and struck a graceful pose like a high-fashion model. All the students' mouths dropped in awe. "Hello, ladies. My name is Ms. Shelly. Welcome to the advanced class, and when we are finished with this class, you will be able to move on the runway just as I did."

Some girls giggled, others shook their heads.

"It's true. I'm just that good," Ms. Shelly said, putting a cotton shirt on over her bustier. "I am so thrilled that you have decided to continue on with your studies. You may very well be on your way to a successful modeling career. In the first class, you learned about skin care and makeup. This class is a lot more intensive. We will focus on your walk on the runway and posing techniques for the camera."

Natasha relaxed into a smile, eager to learn all that the pretty instructor had to offer. She could cast her worries aside; she had faith in Ms. Shelly.

The instructor began the class by re-examining the necessity for good posture and then later moved on to walking techniques on the runway. The last exercise for the day was for each student to get on the runway and practice what she had been studying for the past two hours. Every student was required to place a thick, yellow telephone directory on her head, walk down to the "T" in the runway, pivot and walk back without letting the phone book fall.

Natasha squirmed in her seat the closer it got to her turn. She watched Meagan execute the exercise with perfection

Ms. Shelly grinned. "Natasha, you're next."

Natasha rose slowly from her chair. *Ho ho ho, Green Giant.* She tried not to look into the mirror, but they were plastered on every wall in the narrow, elongated room. Cold sweat stood out on her brow as she made her way to the runway. Natasha felt the other fourteen students' eyes searing through her like a laser, just waiting to rip her insides out. With each step closer to the runway, she thought of basketball. She had never felt this much pressure when she played in front of hundreds of kids. Perhaps she would just stick to playing basketball; at least she didn't feel like the "Green Giant" running down the court. Natasha looked into the mirror; her nose was shining like a new nickel. She wiped the sweat from her forehead and nose, then slid the palm of her hand down her dark denim skirt. She drew in a deep breath and stepped onto the runway where the instructor placed the phone book on her head. Natasha took two steps and the phone book came crashing down, making a loud thump on the runway.

Ms. Shelly placed it on her head again. "That's okay, try it again."

Natasha took a couple of steps, and it fell again.

"Walk lifting your thighs, not on the ball of your toes."

Natasha wiped the sweat from her forehead and dried her hand using her skirt again.

Ms. Shelly placed the phone book on her head a third time. "Look straight ahead, Natasha, not down. If you're looking down, how will the phone book stay balanced?"

Natasha looked into the glass mirror in front of her. She could have easily been mistaken for a Green Bay packer fan wearing a foam cheesehead hat. She took a step and the phone book crashed to the floor.

"Natasha, you work on this at home. And when you come back next week, you should be able to make it down and back," Ms. Shelly said with an encouraging smile.

Natasha nodded, keeping her eyes glued to the beige carpet. To look up would force her to look at her classmates, or worse, herself in those stupid mirrors. She had proved her classmates right—she didn't belong there. No one would hire a tall, clumsy model.

Chapter 4

When Shaniqua awoke from her afternoon nap, her eyes immediately went to the clock. She had ten minutes before Nee Nee would be there to take her over to Brittany's house. Listening carefully, she cracked open her bedroom door. Karen's and Granny's voices carried from the kitchen. Damn it, why ain't she gone! Shaniqua quickly refreshed her makeup and hair, and went downstairs to wait for her ride.

"Oh, look at my baby girl!" Karen cooed, primping her daughter's hair.

Shaniqua wanted to slap her hands down. It was so humiliating to have her come back after ten years and try to act like a mother. Shaniqua gave Granny a kiss goodbye and headed to the front door.

Karen looked hurt. "Wait, what about me? Don't yo' momma get a kiss? I'm the one brought you in the world."

Shaniqua barely touched her mother's sunken jaw. "Bye," she said and slammed the front door shut.

"Girl, don't slam that door like that no mo'!" Granny yelled.

Renee pulled up in front of Brittany's house. In some ways, Nee Nee was like a big sister to Shaniqua because she would give her rides, clothes and advice whenever she needed. Though they were first cousins because their mothers were sisters, they didn't look anything alike. Nee Nee had the rest of the William's family trademark features—dark skin, pug nose and full lips. And like the rest of the family, Nee Nee had dropped out of high school.

Nee Nee slid the gearshift into park and glanced around at the Brown's premises. "Damn girl, I didn't know Brittany's peeps had paper like this?" she said, removing her large Versace sunglasses.

Shaniqua looked around in awe. "Me either."

The house was an elegantly designed six-bedroom home. Two oversized bay windows protruded from the façade. Beautiful white sandstone bricks dressed the exterior of the home.

Nee Nee patted down the loose hairs of her blonde wig. "Damn, I think this the same subdivision the stars live in?"

Shaniqua furrowed her brow. "Who knows, Brittany brags so much."

Nee Nee wrapped her slender hands around the steering wheel, her pumpkin orange fingernails dazzled in the sunlight. "Alright girl, you got a ride home, right?"

Shaniqua shrugged.

Nee Nee dug in her purse and pulled out a stack of singles. "You know I got to work at the club, so take this to call a cab if you need to."

A smile crept across Shaniqua's face. "Thanks."

Nee Nee always gave her money. She had more of it than the whole family. Nee Nee had the best of everything—the most stylish clothes, a new Chrysler 300M and she was getting ready to move out of the apartment she shared with her mom to live by herself.

"Girl, let me know if Brittany has a rich uncle," Nee Nee said, smiling, her gold tooth sparkled. "I don't care if he's old as dirt, blind, crippled or crazy, his money will spend just the same."

Shaniqua hopped out the car and watched Nee Nee drive through the U-shaped driveway. On her way to the front door, Shaniqua noticed the well-manicured flowerbeds and lush landscaping sprawled across at least a couple of acres. Two huge mahogany-stained doors awaited her. She pushed the brass doorbell. It even sounded intimidating, "ding, dong, ding, dong, ching, chong, ching." It had so many different sounds, she lost track. Shaniqua expected a stiff-shirt butler to answer the door. Her heart raced when Mrs. Brown swung open one heavy wooden door. She knew Mrs. Brown didn't care much for her since the car accident last year. She still held her and Natasha responsible for Brittany having been in a coma for weeks.

Mrs. Brown's lips were scrunched, offering the same sour smile as Brittany. "Well, hello, Shaniqua, do come in."

"Hello, Mrs. Brown," Shaniqua said, stepping into the marble foyer. A huge chandelier hung two stories above her head, the kind that she had only seen on MTV Cribs.

"Brittany's expecting you downstairs in the workout room. I'll walk you down. How are you doing?"

Shaniqua glanced around. "Fine." Brittany's house looked like something straight out of a home decorating magazine. Tall, imposing windows permitted sunlight to beam into the immaculate formal living room. Gorgeous mauve colored raw-silk curtains accented the decorative pillows on the white Victorian style furniture. Everything in the room was done in exquisite taste, from the vibrant hand-painted oil canvas on the wall to the Arabesque Lalique crystal vase adorned with fresh flowers.

"So you want to join the cheerleading squad too, huh?"

The sound of Mrs. Brown's voice snapped Shaniqua out of her trance. "Yes, ma'am," she said, marveling at the all-white piano room that she always heard Brittany complain about. A large, sleek white grand piano graced the oversized bay window. Shaniqua would have felt privileged just to be in that room, let alone play.

"I used to cheer for East Lithonia High. I told Brittany I would show you girls a few cheers. Tryouts start next week, right?"

Shaniqua was admiring the beautiful African artwork in the hallway. "Oh, oh, yes, ma'am."

When Shaniqua finally made it downstairs, Brittany was in the middle of the floor, stretching. "Hey, girl," Brittany said, flashing her deep-set dimples. "You ready to get started?"

"I guess."

Mrs. Brown did a few stretches of her own. She was tall and slender, much different from her daughter's stocky frame.

"Uh, Mom, what are you doing?"

Mrs. Brown was bent over into a complicated looking stretch. One of her legs was stretched out while the other one was at a 90-degree angle with her arms looped through. "I'm going to help like I promised."

"Mom, you said you would help us if we needed it. And we don't need help right now. We still have to make up a hello cheer."

"I've got one for you." Mrs. Brown stood up, and then called out, "Hello, ready, ooo-kay." And then began doing strange arm movements and chanting, "Hello, how are you and how do you do, the mighty, mighty Tigers say hello to you."

Shaniqua and Brittany looked at each other, forcing back giggles. "Uh, Mom, that's a little outdated. It's all about competition cheering now."

Mrs. Brown caught her reflection in the mirror across the room. "Excuse me."

Brittany wrapped her arm around her mother's thin waistline. "No offense, Mom, but that cheer is old school. Cheerleaders don't clap like that anymore. It's like this now," Brittany said, cupping her hands together.

"Oh, okay, fine with me. Well, I'll leave you ladies be." Mrs. Brown quickly left the room.

"Ohhh, Brit, you hurt her feelings," Shaniqua said.

"She'll get over it. I just want to do something without her having a hand in it. Mom has to be involved in everything I do. When I played piano, she would sit beside me on the bench. Finally, I had to tell her, 'Mom, I need room to scale the piano'."

Shaniqua offered a weak smile, wishing she had that problem. Karen barely knew she was alive. Before today, it had been at least two years since Shaniqua last saw or heard from her mother. She hated Karen almost as much as she was beginning to hate poverty. Being in Brittany's home made her realize just how poor she and Granny were in their cramped two-bedroom townhouse.

"So, let's get started," Brittany said, thumbing through her notebook. "I already made up some stuff. Tell me what you like."

"Brittany, I'm leaving," Mrs. Brown's voice reverberated over the intercom. "Does Shaniqua have a ride home?"

"Yes, ma'am."

Shaniqua shook her head profusely. "No, I don't."

Brittany put her index finger to her lips. "Alright, bye, Mom."

"Girl, why'd you do that?"

"I'll get you home, chill. Let's work on our routine."

Brittany and Shaniqua practiced chants, arm movements and splits until they were exhausted. The palms of their hands turned red from clapping. Shaniqua collapsed down on the black leather sectional. "I'm tired, and my grandmother's waiting on me. Who's taking me home?"

A mischievous grin spread across Brittany's face. "I am."

"On what? Your back?"

"We've got a Maxima sitting in the fourth garage that no one ever drives. It's my mom's old car."

"Girl, you don't have your license yet."

"So, I've got my permit."

Shaniqua followed Brittany out to the garage. "Alright Brit, can you drive? 'Cause I ain't got time to be getting in an accident."

Brittany sucked in air and let out an exaggerated huff, "Yes, now let's go." Brittany took her time pulling out of the driveway. Her dad was always complaining about how the fourth garage was so much smaller than the other three.

"Your parents let you do this?"

"Well, see, uhm!" Brittany giggled. "My dad's out of town at some type of convention for heart surgeons and my mom's at the shopping mall and won't be home until it closes. Okay, scary Mary?"

Brittany cranked up the music as she cruised down the long driveway. Shaniqua relaxed to Chris Brown's mellow vocals.

"Girl, he is too fine."

"He's alright. You hungry?" Brittany asked.

"Yeah."

Minutes later, Brittany turned into a fast food parking lot where many teens hung out. There was a group of boys standing between an old school Chevelle and a white BMW. Brittany pretended she didn't see them and whipped the car into the parking space with one hand. A loud screeching sound pierced through the music while the driver's side scraped against the ordering booth. Brittany cupped her hand over her mouth. "Oh, no!"

"Just back out slowly, maybe it's not as bad as it sounded."

When Brittany heard kids laughing, she stepped on the gas, jolting the car in reverse. Their heads jerked along. Shaniqua screamed, "What are you doing? I was going to check out the damage!"

Brittany shifted gears and drove off from the cackling sounds of teenagers' laughing. "I'm getting this car home as soon as possible," she said near tears.

"Slow down!"

"You want to drive?" Brittany snapped.

"I don't know how. But I know you need to slow this damn car down before we get into a wreck."

Brittany was angry. Her dad's words kept echoing in her head, "Stop hugging the curves so tightly!" he'd say when he was teaching her to drive. They pulled up in front of Shaniqua's townhouse. Shaniqua hopped out first and ran around to the driver's side. "Uh, I think you need to look at this."

Brittany gasped when she saw the deep metal scrape. "Oh, no. My dad's going to kill me."

"Brit, it was an accident. It's not like you tried to do that."

Brittany blinked down the tears. "I have to get home," she said and drove off.

URBAN GODDESS

Twenty minutes later, Brittany pulled into the driveway, looking for signs that her mom was home, but the house was still dark. The automatic timer hadn't turned on the lights yet. She carefully pulled the car into the garage and darted inside the house. As soon as she heard her mom walk into the kitchen, she hurried down the stairwell, taking two at time. She pulled out a chair and had a seat at the kitchen table. "Hey Mom, how was shopping?"

"Fine. I bought you a new sweater. It's in the smaller bag. How'd cheerleading practice go?"

"Good, we'll be ready for next week."

"I'm sure you'll do great."

Brittany leaned up and kissed her mom. "Well, goodnight."

"Don't forget your sweater."

Brittany grabbed the bag off the countertop and made her way upstairs to her bedroom. She took a seat on the edge of her white four-poster bed and dialed Natasha's number. Brittany pulled a pastel pink sweater out of the bag while waiting for someone to answer.

"Hello?" Natasha said.

"Hey, girl, it's me. What's going on?"

Natasha let out a slight giggle. "I'm getting ready to go out with Stephen."

There was silence.

"Hello? Brittany? Are you there?"

Brittany flung the sweater across the room. "Your parents are letting you go on a date?"

"What's wrong with you? Did you and Shaniqua fall out?"

"No, worse. I wrecked the car."

Natasha gasped. "The new Benz?"

"No, my mom's old Maxima."

"Are you okay? What happened?"

"Yes, I'm fine. But let's just say, the whole driver's side is messed up. I hit the ordering booth at Sonic."

"It can be fixed, right?"

"Tasha, I took the car without my parent's permission."

Natasha gasped. "Girl, why'd you do that?"

"Shaniqua needed a ride home."

"Y'all could have called me. I guess you forgot I got my license in July. When are you going to tell them?"

"I'm not. My soiree is in a few weeks. If my dad finds out, I can cancel my sweet-sixteen party. My mom's already paid for the ballroom, the DJ, and the food."

"Brit, have you lost your entire mind? You can't not tell them. That's being deceitful."

"Nobody ever drives that car anyway, so I'll just tell them after my party. If they find out now, I won't get my new car, they'll probably make me drive that ugly, hideous thing."

"If it were me, I would tell them. Girl, I've got to run. Stephen's picking me up any minute."

"Bye," Brittany said, then crammed a silk mint green pillow over her face.

Chapter 5

Natasha checked herself in the mirror, reapplied lip-gloss and decided to flatiron her hair again. Bone straight, silky smooth hair was in style. The doorbell rang. She glanced at her watch, it was only 7:15; Stephen wasn't supposed to arrive until seven-thirty. Two minutes later, both of her parents appeared in the doorway of her bedroom. "Daddy, what are you doing here?"

"Hey princess, I couldn't let my baby girl go on her first date without seeing her off."

Natasha tried to conceal her smile and nervousness by acting grumpy. "Date? This is not a date, Stephen and I are just friends."

Ms. Harris smoothed down Natasha's hair. "You can call it flying to the moon if you want to, but when a young man picks up a young lady and takes her out for the evening, that's a date."

Mr. Harris pulled his wallet from his pocket. "Here, take this," he said, placing a crisp fifty-dollar bill in Natasha's hand.

A huge smile spread across Natasha's face.

"Thanks, Daddy."

"Wow!" Ms. Harris said. "When I came up, I only got five dollars mad money."

Natasha wrinkled her face. "Mad money?"

Mr. Harris placed his billfold in his back pocket. "This money isn't for you to spend, and especially on him. If things aren't working out and he tries to leave you stranded somewhere, you can catch a cab from just about anywhere he takes you."

"But, Dad, you already met Stephen and you know he's not like that."

"Things don't always go as planned on dates. Some of these young men have other things on their mind, if you know what I mean. Stephen's a boy and I know what it's like to be a sixteen-year-old boy."

Natasha felt suddenly warmer, like a hundred degrees warmer. That was definitely a 5-1-1—more info than necessary. Who wants to imagine their pops being on a date? *Eeeuuw!*

Mr. Harris continued, "Now if he tries anything, you . . ."

"Daddy, I know what to do. God, you guys are treating me like I'm fourteen."

Ms. Harris squeezed her daughter's shoulders. "No, we're teaching you how to conduct yourself like a lady and make the young men treat you with respect." Ms. Harris started snapping her fingers and singing, "R-E-S-P-E-C-T"!

Natasha shook her head. "Uh, no, Mom, leave it to Aretha."

Just then, Neil, her thirteen-year-old brother, ducked his head in Natasha's room and snickered. "Tasha, your prince awaits you."

Natasha smirked. "Shut up, big head!"

"Now, now," Ms. Harris said. "Young ladies don't conduct themselves in such a manner."

Natasha discreetly rolled her eyes and made her way downstairs where Stephen was standing in the foyer admiring the portrait he painted of her last year. "Hey, Stephen," Natasha said casually. "You remember my parents."

"Hello, Mr. Harris, Ms. Harris."

Mr. Harris took a step closer to Stephen. "So, Stephen, what are your plans tonight?"

Natasha held her breath, hoping Stephen wouldn't say the wrong thing.

"Uh, nothing, sir. Uh, a movie and get a bite to eat."

Mr. Harris gripped Stephen's hand into an intensely firm handshake. "Young man, this is my baby girl, take good care of her. And don't drive over the speed limit. I know every cop working tonight in DeKalb County and if I find out . . ."

Ms. Harris interjected, "Stephen, you all have a nice time."

Too afraid to speak, Stephen just nodded.

Natasha pecked her dad's cheek. "I'll call you when I get home tonight."

Mr. Harris's voice was deeper than usual. "Alright, eleven-thirty."

"Good night Mr. and Ms. Harris," Stephen said, holding the front door for Natasha.

Natasha slid into the front of Stephen's parents' car while Stephen held the door open. She stole a quick peek in the sun visor mirror as he walked around the car. They drove along in silence, listening to the radio. Natasha's thoughts were on her parents. She had no intentions on telling her dad about going out with Stephen. For a divorced couple, her parents communicated too well. They had a weird relationship; they were actually cool with one another and strongly believed in co-parenting.

Stephen finally said, "You want to eat first or catch a movie?"

"I'm not really hungry now, so I guess the movie."

An awkward silence fell once more. Natasha wondered if this was Stephen's first real date, too. Then she quickly reminded herself that this was not a date. Dates bring flowers or something. She wondered if maybe her dad had been too hard on him and now maybe Stephen had a change of heart—he didn't even want to go out as friends.

Stephen kept his eyes on the road, refusing to make eye contact. "Tasha, you look nice tonight."

Natasha hid her smile out the passenger side window. "Thanks."

They parked the car and walked up to the movie theater. The smell of hot buttered popcorn greeted them at the door. Natasha could already taste the soft kernel riding the melted butter down her throat. She had gone without popcorn for three years because of her braces. Now that they had been off nearly a year, she seized every opportunity with vengeance.

"You want something?" Stephen asked.

Natasha stole a peek at the concession counter. Time ticked away while she decided if she wanted to look like a pig in front of him, licking her fingers. "No thanks, I'm fine."

During the movie, Stephen's knee pressed against Natasha's. Neither of them made an effort to move it. Natasha felt the soft spark through the rugged fabric of her jeans travel up to her black sweater and into her heart. When the movie ended, they went to Gladys Knight's Chicken & Waffles restaurant. When they finished eating, they still had half an hour until curfew. Stephen took a slow scenic drive, though it was all dark woods, to Natasha's house. He pulled up in front of the house and turned off the ignition.

Natasha looked at him curiously. This is what boys did in the movies, which signified they wanted to kiss. There was no way she was going to kiss him in her mom's driveway. "Do you mind parking a little down the block?"

Stephen cranked the engine while Natasha quickly scanned the area for her dad's car. With her luck, he could be hiding out in the bushes just like the time he hid there one Halloween and when the kids came by to trick or treat, he'd jump out wearing a scary face mask and holding a chainsaw. She relaxed in the seat, glad her father was back at his house.

Suddenly, Natasha felt Stephen's sweaty hand rest on the back of hers. Her heart started pounding.

"Tasha, I had a great time with you tonight."

"Me, too."

"I really like you."

Natasha's eyes widened. Was she supposed to say, me too. *Eeuuww!* How corny. She could not force any words out. She nodded. She knew better than to put her feelings out there first and let him trample on them, the way Jordan did Shaniqua last year. That wasn't going to happen to her.

"You want to be my girl?"

She wondered if a heat wave had suddenly hit Georgia on this late September night. Their breath had fogged up all the windows. Sweat had pressed through the pores on her back, trickling down to her underpants. She had never had a boyfriend, except if you count stupid Dante in seventh grade who never even said hello. That lasted all of two days. Then there was Jeremiah in fifth grade, which lasted until he broke up with her, four days later for Chloe, the whiny gymnast.

Natasha kept her eyes focused on the large white squares in the neighbor's garage door, "Yes," she finally responded.

Stephen exhaled noisily, which prompted both of them to release nervous laughter. Stephen moved closer to Natasha. She stole a quick peek to see if her nosey brothers were looking out the windows. Though, they wouldn't be able to see through the fogged over windows. Stephen placed his lips on hers. They were soft, sweet like. They locked mouths in a warm embrace, dissolving time into nothingness. Natasha didn't know how long they had kissed; she was lost in oblivion, somewhere between Stephen being a great kisser to her body reacting to the excitement. Natasha promptly pulled away and whispered goodnight.

Chapter 6

Monday after school, the gymnasium clamored with chants, laughter and nervous energy. Shaniqua and Brittany were both excited to have their first official cheerleading tryout. "Dang, it must be at least a hundred girls here," Shaniqua said, sizing up their competition. "Everybody and their momma wants to cheerlead. How many spots are open?"

Brittany slipped off her maroon sweat pants. "Six on varsity and twelve on JV. But girl, you can't worry about that. I just hope they don't ask me to do the splits or hurkey jump."

"You mean like this," Shaniqua said, dropping down into a Chinese splits with the ease of a trained gymnast.

Brittany flung her long ponytail around. "Show off! Hurry up and get dressed."

Shaniqua planted her hands on her little curvy hips. "I'm wearing this." She tugged at her black short shorts and pulled the bottom of her black fitted tank top.

"Shaniqua, that looks stank! Your booty cheeks are nearly hanging out the bottom of your shorts."

"Brittany, please. Most of the girls on the squad are petite and have cute shapes, so I'm going to show them I fit in with them, 'cause I know my body is slammin'. Don't hate. Oh, I will be a flyer on the squad. So that little Hispanic chick, Mina, Mia, or whatever her name is, needs to step aside."

Coach Felder, the varsity cheerleading coach, entered the gym and the noisy chatter immediately died down. She could easily be mistaken for one of the cheerleaders on the squad. She wore her hair in a ponytail just like the cheerleaders, dressed in the same practice uniform and had the same cheesy, wide mouth smile typical of most cheerleaders. Coach Felder explained what would be expected for tryouts and then introduced the varsity squad girls to teach the routine. The line of varsity cheerleaders stretched out across the length of the gym, divided everyone into groups of four and then passed out tryout numbers to secure on each girl's shirt.

Shaniqua was relieved that she didn't have Hailey from homeroom instructing her. She was too annoying, over-the-top peppy, sickening peppy. She and Brittany lucked out with Amber, a quiet senior. Amber walked them slowly through the tryout routine. Shaniqua caught on quickly and proceeded to help Brittany and some of the other girls learn it. Shaniqua was a natural, she had been dancing around the house for as long as she could remember and cheerleading wasn't much different except the movements were much stiffer. At times, she wanted to rub Brittany's skin to see if the color would come off. For a black girl, Brittany totally lacked dance rhythm.

After they practiced the dance routine, Coach Felder

instructed the varsity cheerleaders to pull out the blue mats so they could tumble. Coach Felder made it clear to everyone that in order to make varsity, you had to be able to complete a backhand spring. Shaniqua executed hers with ease. She had been doing it for years. Poor inner-city children tumbled in the grass for fun when there was nothing else to play with. Brittany struggled to do a good cartwheel.

On Thursday morning, the split of daylight seeped into Shaniqua's bedroom, waking her. She quickly emptied her bladder and sneaked out of the bathroom without flushing the toilet, trying not to alert her mother that she was awake. Shaniqua tiptoed back to her bed, glancing at the bold, red numbers, 6:02, on the clock. She pulled the covers up around her neck, she still had thirteen minutes before the alarm sounded. Suddenly, she heard a tapping at the door. Shaniqua knew it wasn't Granny—Granny always tapped very softly, then bulldozed her way in. Shaniqua closed her eyes and pretended to be asleep.

"Nique, Nique," her mother said in a raspy voice.

Nique, Nique ricocheted between Shaniqua's ears. Why was she calling her that as if they were really mother and daughter? That's what real mothers do, give their children pet names. At the age of sixteen, Karen was a little late.

Her mother pushed open the door. "Nique, Nique, time for school."

Shaniqua slowly removed the faded blue sheet from over her face. Karen's presence was nauseating; she wished her mother would simply go back to whatever hellhole she crawled out of. Every morning and night, Karen came into her bedroom trying to strike up a conversation. Even if Shaniqua did have something going on, she sure as hell wasn't about to tell Karen, a stranger.

"I made breakfast. You comin' downstairs to eat while it's hot?"

Shaniqua slipped on the pair of dingy footies at the end of her bed and scooted past her mother standing in the doorway. "Thanks," she said, though she hadn't ever remembered Karen cooking even a boiled egg. They had always lived with Granny and Granny always did all the cooking. She wondered if her mother even knew how to cook.

Shaniqua made her way down to the kitchen. Some mornings, the kitchen looked like a circus with all the brightly colored fruit plastered on the walls. Everything in the kitchen had some type of fruit on it. The wallpaper had grapevines sprouting wildly across the walls. The curtains were blue, with lime and lemon Ballard print. Granny had succeeded in overdoing the fruit theme. Each year, she would add on—a new towel here or plastic banana there. Shaniqua grabbed a plate decorated with painted red currants from the cabinet.

Granny eyed Shaniqua suspiciously. "You wash yo' hands this morning, chile?"

"Yes, ma'am."

"I didn't hear no water running."

"Granny, I did. I promise," Shaniqua said, scooping the eggs out of the skillet. "What's this?"

"Your favorite, sunnyside-up, the way you used to eat them when you were a little kid," Karen said.

Shaniqua shot Karen a scorching look, her eyes burned with disgust. Fighting fiercely to hold back the tears, a tiny voice within cried, Why didn't you love me enough to stay? She shoved the plate down on the kitchen table and ran upstairs to get dressed for school.

Shaniqua dressed quickly and closed her bedroom door tightly behind her, letting the sound of the slamming door communicate for her. She hoped it was sending a strong message to Karen to stay the hell out of her room when she wasn't there. Since Karen had been there, nothing was ever in the same place. Shaniqua left for school without saying goodbye to anyone. Her mind was on cheerleading tryouts, the only good thing in her life.

She and Brittany had practiced their routine all week and now she was ready to perform. After school, Shaniqua quickly made her way into the gym; nervous energy loomed in the atmosphere. All the girls spoke in hushed tones and let out sporadic bits of worried laughter. Coach Felder announced the order in which the girls would perform and then retreated to a seat behind an oblong table alongside three other judges. Shaniqua's heart did a slight dip when she realized Hailey was a judge. She drew in a deep breath and tried to relax when she exhaled. She had nothing to worry about she was a good cheerleader.

No, she was one of the best, she decided. She was limber, her jumps had a lot of height, and she could tumble.

The first girls up, took to the floor and began doing the routine. Brittany and Shaniqua offered one another knowing looks. Brittany pursed her lips. "Not! Their arms are flimsy like waving flags. Next!"

Another set of girls performed. Their arms made nice crisp movements, but they didn't have the dance routine down. One of the judges challenged them to do a backhand spring. The first girl performed a cartwheel. Someone chuckled. Next, her partner executed an awesome backhand spring. Her feet were still together when she landed. Shaniqua bit her bottom lip—that was one less spot for her on varsity.

"Brittany Brown and Shaniqua Williams?" one of the judges called out.

Brittany and Shaniqua stood in front of the judges, offering one another encouraging smiles. The music sprung them into action. They kept time with the beats and smiled on cue. Next, they bellowed out enthusiastic cheers in low voices, using their diaphragms. As soon as they finished, the judges thanked them.

When they were safely outside the gym, Shaniqua and Brittany jumped around, hugging one another. "We did good, girl!" Shaniqua said. "But, I wonder why they didn't ask us to do our jumps or tumbling."

Brittany shrugged. "Don't worry, I can tell they liked us by the way they were looking at us. We are in like sin—well, not like sin, but we in!"

Shaniqua couldn't wait to get home to tell Granny how well she and Brittany performed. When she entered the house, there was no aroma floating through the house, only the smell of a sturdy disinfectant. Usually, Granny was in the kitchen cooking dinner or baking a pie or cake for someone at church. Shaniqua ran into the kitchen, dropped her backpack on the watermelon throw rug and looked around, then sprinted up the stairs to Granny's bedroom where Granny was sitting on the edge of her bed, thumbing through a pile of papers. "Hey baby, how was yo cheerleadin' tryout?"

"Pretty good."

"Nobody in this family ever did anything for the school. You gonna be the first to finish."

There was something strange in Granny's voice. Shaniqua took a seat beside her. "Is everything okay?"

Granny's eyes were red and watery. Her shoulders drooped in sadness. "Yes, well, no," she said, rising from her bed. "Part of our rent money is missin'."

Shaniqua scrunched her face in confusion. "Missing? How could it be missing? You keep it on your dresser every month until Mr. Clark comes to pick it up. There's nobody here but us."

A loud creak sounded from downstairs, signaling that someone was coming through the front door.

"How much is missing?" Shaniqua said.

"Three hundred dollars."

"Three hundred!" Shaniqua shot up from the bed, "Oh, hell no. No, she didn't!" She darted downstairs to the front door. "Karen, our rent money is missing."

"Who in the hell do you think you calling Karen? I'm yo' momma."

The stench of alcohol mingled with the stale scent of cigarettes sent waves of revulsion coursing through Shaniqua as Karen got in her face. Shaniqua glowered at her mother, her tawny eyes smoldering with fire. "Where's the money?"

"I don't have no money. I don't know what you talking about."

Shaniqua stared blankly into Karen's eyes, the two shiny black balls of nothingness. She wanted to slap the living hell out of her for stealing from her own mother. "Bull!"

Granny made her way down the stairs. "Wait a minute, chile, this is a Christian household. We don't use that kind of language here."

Shaniqua was so hot, she wanted to cry. Who would want to steal from Granny? Granny had been the backbone and savior to everyone in the family. A tear streaked down Shaniqua's cheek. More threatened to follow. God only knows where she would have ended up if it had not been for her grandmother. Shaniqua wiped her face with the back of her hand and then dried it on her black velour sweat pants. "Karen, where's the money?"

Karen's eyes widened, her face twisted into a demonic glare. "Call me Karen again! I brought you in this world, and I'll take you out!"

"Alright, that's enough from both of y'all! Lawda

mercy," Granny said.

"Granny, she took the money. Ain't nobody else in this house but the three of us," Shaniqua said, then turned back to face Karen. "Why don't you just leave!"

"You leave! This is my damn momma's house!"

"Chile, go on upstairs, I'll handle this," Granny said, her voice now rather calm.

Shaniqua stomped up the stairs. "That's pretty damn lowdown to steal from yo' own momma! You're a poor excuse for a daughter, not to mention a mother!" Before she reached the top of the stairs, she heard quick footsteps pounding up the stairs.

"What! I'll beat you down!" Karen said, charging at her daughter, one hand heading toward Shaniqua's face. She tried to duck, but it was too late. Karen's ring grazed Shaniqua's temple as her hand struck her left cheek with so much force it knocked Shaniqua against the wall.

Too dazed to make a sound, Shaniqua picked herself up and scurried into the bathroom, quickly locking the door. She stared at her face in disbelief. Examining the red swell of hatred against her skin prompted her to cry aloud. "I hate you!" Rage now fueled her. She no longer felt the pain in her face; it had traveled to a more remote place—her soul. Everything in her little body told her to hurt Karen. She looked around the bathroom for a weapon. She inspected the linen closet, found nothing. She bent down to search underneath the sink, checking for loose pipes. There were none. Shaniqua noticed an open canister of Comet. *Perfect. I'll show this witch! I hate her!* She knew the cleanser would not kill her, but at least she could throw it in her eyes, letting it burn the hell out of them. Shaniqua sprang up from the floor, catching an unexpected glimpse of herself in the mirror. She no longer saw the bruise on her face, but something much more painful: the eyes of her mother, large, brown, and almond-shaped, piercing through her, her mother's face, frowning, with thin lips and downcast eyes. Unable to bear the image; Shaniqua closed her eyes. Tears cascaded down her pallid face. She began to sob, the noise tearing out of her. She hurled the canister at her reflection, splattering Comet powder everywhere.

Chapter 7

That night Shaniqua tossed and turned, but sleep would not come. Her faced throbbed with pain, her heart with hatred. Instead of thinking about Karen, she focused on the only bright spot in her life. In the morning, she would be a Miller Grove Vikings cheerleader. Her shapely, petite frame would look so cute in the snug fitting maroon uniform. She would gather her micro braids into a high ponytail and wrap pretty maroon and gold ribbons around it. Everyone knew that cheerleaders were the premier girls to date in high school. Now, all the boys, especially Jordan, would want to date her just to be seen with a cheerleader and she could play hard to get. Unless of course, there was a cute jock—then they could become the cute couple around the school whom everybody knew and loved. Visions of her cheering at the football games comforted her and settled her into a deep slumber.

In the early morning, Shaniqua stepped off the school bus into the moist, damp air, the cool breeze stinging her bruise as she hurried into school. She hoped and prayed her concealer would hide the traces of hatred on her face.

She had no plans to tell her friends about her mother. They would never know her reality, no one would.

Shaniqua dashed into the building and down the hallway where the results would be posted on the cheerleading coach's door. A long line of girls checking to see who had made it formed a large, noisy crowd. Some girls were sniffling, while others jumped around ecstatically. A stringy-haired brunette crouched against the wall, her hands pressed tightly over her eyes, crying like a hungry baby. Shaniqua knew that the girl didn't deserve to be on varsity or JV, because she couldn't keep time with the steps.

Shaniqua stood across the hall, waiting for the crowd to thin. When she finally made her way over to the list, she closed her eyes and drew in a deep calming breath. Seven names were on the sheet for varsity. She scrolled slowly; Brittany Brown was second. Shaniqua smiled because she knew that if Brittany made it, then so had she. When Shaniqua read the last name, Stacy Washington, she gasped in disbelief. Her name was not on the varsity list, not even as an alternate. Too flabbergasted to cry, she stared at the names of girls who had made it. She was a better cheerleader than all of them, including Brittany. Shaniqua moved over to the junior varsity list and started at the top and worked her way down, annunciating each syllable, until she reached the last name, Miranda Thomas. Her name had been omitted there, too. How could they do that to her? An ache swelled in her throat, preventing her from screaming at the top of her lungs. Hot, angry tears threatened to erupt like lava from a volcano, but when she heard Natasha and Brittany approaching, she quickly blinked them back and grinned. "Brit, you made it!"

"For real?"

Brittany and Natasha closed in on the list. Brittany jumped up and down, while Natasha wrapped her arm around Shaniqua. "I'm sorry, girl. Are you okay?"

"Yeah. It's not that big of a deal. I've got to get to homeroom. See you guys at lunch," she said, then hurried down the hall. Tears welled up and this time she couldn't stop them. With her head hung low, she scurried into the girls' bathroom, ducked into the very last stall and pressed her fingers over her eyes until the tardy bell summoned students to class. Shaniqua didn't care about being late today. She continued sitting there, crouched over the commode, pouring her feelings into tears. She cried about cheerleading, her mother, the rent money, her life.

Shaniqua slumped in the chair in English 3 doodling dollar signs on a clean sheet of paper, oblivious to Mr. Evans' discussion of *Lord of the Flies*. Shaniqua tried her best to focus, but she just didn't care about a bunch of little boys stranded on an island. She was stranded in the inner city. Granny needed rent money. The clock ticked while her mind roamed. Maybe she could quit school altogether and get a job. It wasn't like she was doing great in school. She was just barely passing. She had always been just barely passing for the past several years. So, dropping out and working instead wouldn't be a bad idea. It would relieve a lot of financial pressure. She could help pay the bills, buy herself and Granny a cell phone, her own clothes, maybe even a car, just like Nee Nee had done. Maybe she could ask Nee Nee to lend her the money and tell her it was from someone else. She knew Granny would never take Nee Nee's money; she called it, "The devil's money."

Two years ago, Shaniqua and Granny were sitting in the dark because the electricity bill hadn't been paid. Luckily, it had been in the springtime. They ate and bathed by candlelight for three days until Granny's social security check arrived. But this time was different. Where would they go if the landlord put them out for non-payment? Nowhere. Granny hardly ever talked to her other daughter, Kathy, Nee's Nee's mother, even though they lived two blocks away. Granny said they were into too much "devilment."

Shaniqua was deep in thought when she discovered Mr. Evans standing over her desk, watching. He was a short, stockily built teacher. He would be considered handsome, if he wasn't so old—mid to late 30's. He cleared his throat. "Shaniqua, this is English class, not Art."

She sighed, slapped her notebook closed and turned her focus to the front of the classroom. She had always heard kids cracking on one another, "You so broke you can't pay attention." Now that felt like her life for real.

Just before class was about to end, a slow, deliberate smile crept across her face. She had found a solution to her and Granny's problems. Jordan Kelley. Mr. Evans banged a plastic ruler against the desktop, snapping Shaniqua back to the present. "Ms. Williams, see me after class," he said, then continued with the class discussion.

She knew Mr. Evans was going to give her a good scolding. He was an even-tempered, jovial man, but didn't take kindly to students, especially African Americans, failing his class. As one of the few African American male teachers in the school, he felt it was his sole responsibility to talk to students about the importance of getting an education. If Mr. Evans had an African American student pulled off to the side in the hallway, everyone knew what he was saying. He always started his lecture the same way. "Statistics say you're going to fail." He was well known and liked around the school by teachers and students alike. Almost all the boys towered over him, but none of them ever talked back to him; Mr. Evans held the school's football rushing record.

Chaos erupted in the halls when the lunch bell sounded. Shaniqua's heart palpitated as the classroom emptied, leaving her to contend with him alone. "Come up here, young lady," Mr. Evans said.

"Yes, sir." Shaniqua took her time gathering her books.

"What's going on with you?"

"Nothin'."

"You haven't turned in any homework and you don't participate in the class discussions."

Shaniqua thought of using her mother as an excuse

for failing, but that would be too embarrassing.

"Statistics say you're going to be a baby's momma, with baby momma drama living in the projects on welfare. Is that what you want for your life? Somebody telling you how much money you can have every month or telling you where you can live. That's just another form of slavery. Is that how you see yourself?"

Shaniqua shook her head, but the truth was, she never gave it any thought. All she knew was that she could do hair to earn a living.

"If you want to have a good life, then education is the key." Mr. Evans began. "If you want to do nothing with your life, then keep on doing what you're doing and you're going to keep on getting what you're getting, and right now, that's an 'F'! I've been where you are, so don't think I don't know what I'm talking about. I grew up in Capital Homes in downtown Atlanta. I sold dope just to buy groceries for my momma. But ain't, and yes, I said, ain't, but two ways you headed when you get into that stuff—one, six feet under or two, behind bars. Do better than your parents did. Make better life choices. Just because the people around you may not strive to do anything with their lives, don't mean you have to do the same thing. So you think about that."

"Yes, sir," she said and hurried out of his class.

❧

Before heading to the cafeteria, Shaniqua made a quick stop in the bathroom to re-apply concealer to her cheek. Satisfied that her friends would not be able to see the bruise, she sat down at their table and began picking over her food as usual, listening to Brittany carry on about whom to invite to her sweet sixteen soiree. Shaniqua studied her dried out chicken patty, waiting for the opportune time to tell them that she was going to quit school.

"My mom said the printer will have the invitations ready on Friday, and we're dropping them in the mail Saturday morning. And the other people, I'll bring their invitations with me to school on Monday. My party's going to be off the chain!"

Natasha and Shaniqua exchanged knowing looks; they both wanted Brittany to shut up.

"I'm going to invite all the cheerleaders on the varsity squad, but JV can hang it up. No underclassmen allowed! Too bad, so sad! Tasha, are you bringing your new man?"

Natasha smiled at the thought of Stephen. "I don't know. I don't think he's into parties."

Brittany turned to Shaniqua. "And who are you bringing, Ms. Thang?"

"I ain't got no money for a freakin' formal gown!"

"My theme is Hollywood Glamour, but that doesn't mean you have to be formally dressed. My mother had my gown made because I'm the hostess." Brittany turned to

Natasha, "Oh and yes, I will be rocking a tiara."

Shaniqua hunched and stared off in the distance. Brittany's party was the last thing on her mind. She and Granny needed money for shelter. Shaniqua scanned the lunchroom for Jordan but didn't see him.

"So, who's the birthday girl's date?" Natasha asked.

"Girl, please. My parents aren't letting me have a date for my own party, can you believe that? They are such dolts!" Brittany shrugged. "But I don't care as long as they get my new Lexus."

Natasha cupped her hand over her mouth. "You're kidding, right? I don't believe you're getting a Lexus?"

Brittany gave an imperious smirk. "Oh, believe it!"

Shaniqua toyed with her mashed potatoes. "What did your parents do about the dent in the car?"

"Nothing. I'm not telling them. Are you crazy? They would cancel the party, Christmas, and the rest of my life!"

"Hey, guys, my fashion show's this weekend at Lenox mall in front of Macy's at one p.m. Be there or be square."

"Aren't we all going together?" Brittany asked.

Natasha looked apologetically at her friends. "Well, Stephen is..."

Brittany interrupted, "All you ever talk about is Stephen. Stephen this, Stephen that."

Shaniqua smiled for the first time. "Sounds like somebody's been sipping hateorade!"

"I'm not hating, I'm just saying, that's all she ever talks about now. Before it used to be us, now that Natasha has a man, she doesn't have time anymore."

Natasha frowned. "It's not even like that. I was going

to tell you that I'm going with my parents and that Stephen is coming along, and if we had enough room, you guys could come, too."

"Whatever, Tasha, I've got to go. I'll check my cheerleading schedule and see if I'm available," Brittany said in a huff.

The bell concluded the lunch period.

Shaniqua shook her head. "Girl, don't let Brittany bother you. She's just jealous because she ain't got a man."

"I'm not thinking about her. Sorry about cheerleading."

"Psssst, I'm over it!"

Natasha studied the look in her friend's eyes. They were the saddest that she had ever seen. "Is everything okay?"

Shaniqua nodded.

"No, Shaniqua. I've known you since the third grade, I know when something's wrong."

Silence loomed between them while the cafeteria clamored with noise. Natasha reached across the table to touch Shaniqua's arm. "You pregnant again?"

"No!" Shaniqua said. "I'm thinking of quitting school."

Natasha chuckled.

"I'm serious, Tasha."

"Over cheerleading? Girl, it is not that serious."

"It has nothing to do with cheerleading."

Natasha's smile faded when she realized Shaniqua was serious. "Girl, you can't do that. That would be the worst thing you could do. Why do you want to drop out?"

"Cause."

Natasha glanced at the clock mounted against the dull yellow wall. "We have to get to class, but promise me you won't quit before we talk about it some more."

Shaniqua nodded.

"I'm serious," Natasha said and stuck out her pinky finger. "Pinky promise."

Shaniqua wrapped her pinky around Natasha's finger, "I promise, and don't tell Brittany."

"I won't. See you later," Natasha yelled down the hall.

Chapter 8

When the last bell rang, Shaniqua raced over to Jordan's locker where he was leaning against his locker laughing with his friends. Her nerves were raw. She didn't really want to go down there and talk to him in front of everyone. But she had to. He was the only person who could help her. Shaniqua approached him cautiously. "Jordan, can I talk to you for a moment?"

All four boys turned around to look at her. "Oh snap, damn dog, you the man," one of them said. "Damn, you puttin' it down like that again?" another one said.

Jordan smiled. "I'll holla !" he said, and dapped his friends goodbye. "What's up, Shorty?"

Shaniqua smiled bashfully. "Well, remember that money?"

"Oh, you mean this?" he said pulling an even larger wad out of his pocket than before.

"I need it."

Jordan grinned. "What you gone do for me?"

"Huh?"

"What you gone do for me? Ain't nothin' free."

"What?" Shaniqua couldn't believe what she was hearing. She smiled. "Are you playing?"

"Hell naw! You got to give up somethin'."

Shaniqua's smile vanished. Her heart pounded in her chest. She was growing angrier by the second. She studied his bloodshot eyes. He smelled like marijuana. She hated him. He was rotten to the core. "Screw you, Jordan!"

He cackled. "Screw you, trick!"

"You gone get yours," she said and then stormed away with angry tears in her eyes.

"I'm here now. What you wanna do?" he yelled down the hallway.

Shaniqua walked briskly from the bus stop to Granny's front door, pleading with God that Karen would not be there. She would have gone by her Aunt Kathy's apartment to talk with Nee Nee, but she desperately needed to get home to take her medicine. The doctor had told her any type of stress could cause an outbreak. Shaniqua didn't think that she was really stressed out, but the lesions on her vaginal area were itching and burning. She needed to find relief. After researching more about the disease last year on the Internet, it made her feel better to know that eighty million people also suffered from genital herpes. However, today it was of little consequence, she was feeling the pain alone.

Shaniqua slowly stuck the key into the lock and turned the knob. Holding her breath, she cocked a critical ear to the door. No one was speaking. She heard noise in the kitchen—the kitchen table was creaking from someone leaning on it. It had to be Granny. She peeked down the hallway to see if Karen was sitting in there, too. She wasn't. Silently, she thanked God and yelled "hello" to Granny while making a mad dash to her bedroom. She searched for her medications in her top dresser drawer. Finding both the pills and the ointment, Shaniqua hurried into the bathroom, locked the door and used her hand as a cup to gather water. Next, she sat on the toilet seat and grabbed the mirror to have a look. Red puffy sores had enveloped the area. She used a cotton swab to apply the ointment as the doctor suggested; otherwise, she would run the risk of transmitting it to another area, or worst, someone else. When she finished, she washed her hands three times, scrubbing ferociously and then dried them on a raggedy hand towel. Angrily, she stormed out of the bathroom and into her bedroom. She picked up the telephone and dialed 9-1-1. An operator answered. "Hello, yes, I would like to report a drug dealer."

"I'll connect you, one moment," the operator said.

"DeKalb County Narcotics, Detective Ashford speaking how may I help you?"

"There's a boy at my school dealing drugs."

"What kind of drugs, ma'am?"

"Crack, marijuana, I don't know. All I know is he has a whole bunch of money and a lot of people hang out by his car after school. I go to Miller Grove High. His name's Jordan Kelley. He drives a blue '68 Impala."

"What's the license plate number?"

"I don't know."

"Can I have your name and call back number in case I need more information?"

Shaniqua gasped and then slammed the phone down. She hoped they didn't trace the call. She opened the bedroom door slowly, listening for movement in the other rooms. There was none. She made her way downstairs to the kitchen where Granny was sitting at the table, peeling sweet potatoes. She kissed her grandmother's cheek. "Hi, Granny."

"Hi baby, how you?"

"Good."

"You got homework?"

"No, ma'am. Where's Karen?" Shaniqua said, looking into the pantry for a snack.

"Chile, if you don't get over to the sink and wash yo' hands, you better!"

Shaniqua walked over to the kitchen sink, the checkered green and white linoleum crackling underneath her weight. "Sorry. Where's Karen?"

"I don't know. I haven't seen her since yesterday. I 'spect she's gone off again."

"Good! I hate it when she's here."

"Chile, you watch yo' mouth. That's yo' momma. God ain't gave you but one momma. I can't help the way she is. Lawd knows I tried, but you must respect her as yo' momma."

Shaniqua sighed. She and Granny had had this

conversation every time Karen ran off. How was she supposed to respect a mother who was trying to fight her as if she was her enemy on the street? Though, the pain in Shaniqua's cheek didn't compare to the pain in her heart. Karen had snatched her heart out of her body when she left ten years ago, now she was stomping on it with spiked shoes. Shaniqua found herself tuning Granny out. Her emotions were rampant—from anger and bitterness to heartache and sadness. There was nothing new that Granny could say. Shaniqua studied the tin sculptured apples and grapes hinged against the wall above the sink, cringing. "Granny, I forgot, I need to study for a test."

"Oh, okay, baby. Dinner be ready after while. We havin' sweet potato pie for dessert."

Schoolwork was the last thing on Shaniqua's mind as she made her way upstairs. She was failing English because she hadn't turned in any homework or classroom assignments since the first day of school and she had a D average in Algebra 2. Brittany and Natasha were both in Calculus. She was always behind them. She could never compete with them; they always had someone pushing them to excel. Shaniqua had no one. Granny often asked if she had homework, but never verified it. And whenever she brought home bad grades, Granny said, "I know you can do better," and that was the extent of it.

The urge to write was overwhelming. Shaniqua searched her backpack for her composition notebook. She would never admit this to anyone, especially Mr. Evans, her English teacher, but writing was therapeutic for her. She could lose herself in her thoughts without anyone placing judgment on her or her thoughts. They were hers and hers alone. She turned to a blank page and began writing, letting her feelings and thoughts flow unequivocally, without trying to control them. They poured ferociously onto the paper until she found herself scribbling *I hate her! I hate her! I hate her! I never want to be like her. She's a nobody. A nothing.*

Tears streamed down her pallid face. Moaning like a three-year-old child with a scraped kneecap, Shaniqua curled into a fetal position on her bed, and placed the pillow over her mouth to muffle the noise. Her pain was raw and the only way to ease it was to let it out in the form of crying. After ten minutes, her pillow was moist with a fusion of tears, snot, and slobber. When she removed the pillow, a wave of embarrassment washed over her; she wiped the mixture off her face using a t-shirt that was lying on the bed, and smiled. She smiled through tear-stained eyes, grateful to God for her tears; not all His creatures have the ability to relieve sudden hurt with quick tears. She reached for the phone and called Nee Nee.

The night air was chilly while Shaniqua sat on the little front porch waiting for Nee Nee, staring into the dark sky. The stars looked peaceful like mini marshmallows swimming in hot chocolate. Startled by the sound of Nee Nee's car pulling up to the curb in front of the house, Shaniqua looked out to the street and made her way to the car. "Thanks for coming."

Nee Nee grimaced. "I'm on my way to work, what's this about Shaniqua?"

"I needed to talk to you about something, but I don't want Granny to find out."

"Get in the car. Why didn't you just come over to my house?"

A long pause followed. Shaniqua was searching for the right answer. She didn't know if she could trust Nee Nee to keep her mouth shut.

"Shaniqua!" Nee Nee snapped.

"Because . . ." Shaniqua said, staring out the car window. "I don't want to see Karen."

"Why?"

Shaniqua let out a loud huff. "Never mind, I need a favor."

"How much now, Shaniqua? You need to get a damn job."

"I know! That's what I want to talk to you about. I need three hundred dollars."

"Three hundred dollars! The hell you say!"

"I'll pay you back. I just need it."

"Damn, you pregnant again?" Nee Nee asked, shaking her head. "I told you this was going to happen. Why in the hell you keep messing around without protection?"

Tears welled up in Shaniqua's eyes, then cascaded down her face. An ache in her throat swelled almost to the point of suffocation. She would never be able to live down what happened between her and Jordan, not at school nor home. "I'm not pregnant!" she shouted.

Nee Nee's head whipped around at her outburst. "Damn girl, you don't have to holler!"

"I'm just sick of everyone thinking that way about me. I'm just tired!" Shaniqua let out a high-pitched squeal. "Tired, tired, tired!" Shaniqua yelled, wiping the wetness from her cheeks.

Through peripheral vision, each cousin watched the other. Both, too paralyzed with discomfort, offered nothing. Shaniqua let out infrequent sniffles while the atmosphere remained intensely quiet.

Nee Nee cranked the engine.

"Wait, I'm sorry. I just got a lot on my mind. Somebody stole some of the rent money from Granny."

"For real? Ain't nobody been there but Auntie Karen!"

Shaniqua offered a slow nod.

"That's jacked up." Nee Nee said. "Give me a couple of days."

A small sigh escaped from Shaniqua. "Thanks. There's something else."

Nee Nee frowned.

"I'm going to quit school and get a job at the club where you work."

"Oh hell no! Have you lost your damn mind? What the hell you mean dropping out of school!"

"You did it!" Shaniqua retorted.

"I regret it, too. You think I want to do this. Yeah, the money's good. But you don't know everything I have to do to get it 'cause I don't tell you everything."

"But Granny needs help now!"

"Don't quit school, Shaniqua. I'm telling you. That would be your worst mistake, not to mention you'll break Granny's heart. You're all she ever talks about—how proud she is of you and how you so much different from the rest of the family."

"I ain't even doing that good in school. We need money now!"

Nee Nee put the gearshift in drive, but kept her foot on the brake. "Go get a little job after school. Flip burgers or something. I'll be back with the money in a couple of days."

Shaniqua got out of the car. "Thanks," she said as Nee Nee peeled off, burning rubber.

Chapter 9

Saturday morning, Natasha paced back and forth waiting for Stephen to arrive while her family dressed upstairs. So much was riding on her fashion show debut at Lenox Square, the hottest mall in Atlanta. If she fell on stage, she would be committing social suicide and would never be able to live it down. People in the entertainment industry hung out there. The Atlanta Hawks and Falcons players shopped there. On any given day, there was destined to be a celebrity of some sort passing through.

Natasha playfully struck various poses in the mirror in the downstairs hallway to ensure that she looked good from all angles. She hated to admit it, but she spent a lot of time in front of the mirror. It had become her new best friend. On the weekends, she would easily pass hours like minutes, practicing her runway swagger, camera techniques or testing new makeup and hairstyles. When the doorbell rang, Natasha was already standing in the front foyer. "Hey, Stephen," she said as she swung open the door.

"Wow, you look beautiful," he said, leaning in for a kiss.

Natasha offered her cheek. There was no way she was going to kiss her boyfriend in her mother's house while her mother was home.

"So, are you ready?" Stephen said.

Natasha offered an uncertain smile. "As ready as I'll ever be. I just hope I don't trip."

The phone on the foyer table rang. Natasha grabbed it. "Hello?"

"Tasha, can you pick me up?"

"Well, hello to you, too, Shaniqua. What's wrong with you?"

"I'm sitting here dressed, waiting on Brittany and I can't get in touch with her. Her cell phone isn't on."

"Shaniqua, I'm so sorry, but our car is full."

Stephen interrupted, "Does Shaniqua need a ride? I can pick her up."

Natasha smiled. "Would you, Stephen?"

"Sure, no problem."

"Shaniqua, Stephen will pick you up. I'll give him your address, and I'll meet you guys there because I've got to get going."

Natasha said goodbye to Shaniqua and quickly jotted down Shaniqua's address and directions to her home.

Waiting behind the heavy red curtain backstage,

Natasha's nerves were raw. She hoped the dress shields were going to protect the outfit from her sweaty armpits. When the music began, the curtains parted and the lights blazed against the silver and white backdrop. Meagan, the tall blonde, went first. A thunder of cheers resonated, igniting anxiety once more. Natasha wiped her forehead with the palm of her hand and then slid it down the new hot pink cotton pants. The sweat meshed through the fabric, creating a wet spot on her thigh. She stole a quick peek at the stage exit door. Her feet threatened to carry her over there, but Ms. Shelly glared at her to go. Natasha drew in a deep breath and listened to the music's rhythm. It calmed her nerves. She stepped one foot on the runway and then another. Her awkward walk slowly turned into a sashay. Natasha made it to the end of the runway, struck a sassy pose and the crowd roared. With each change of clothes, she grew more confident, gliding with a strong pelvic lead, her hips seemed to arrive before the rest of her. She moved across the platform like a true fashion model working the catwalk. By the end of the show, Natasha no longer resembled the girl that everyone knew. She had transformed into a high fashion runway model.

Chapter 10

Sunday morning, all around her Shaniqua heard the saints' voices singing along with the choir an old spiritual while she watched the deacons watching the mound of money pass from person to person, pew to pew. It was a shameful thought, but she wished she had the church offerings for herself and Granny. Two days had passed and she hadn't heard from Nee Nee.

Reverend Cosby rose from the leather throne-like chair, and nodded to the choir, signaling that it was his time. He was a tall and imposing figure in a rich, purple robe. "Let's go to the old testament, the Book of Numbers, Chapter Thirty."

Shaniqua dozed.

"Faith" the pastor roared, ". . . can move mountains." A host of "Amens" and "Hallelujahs" erupted from the congregation, waking Shaniqua from her nap. She looked at Granny who was standing in the next row with her hands raised in the air.

Reverend Cosby continued, "Faith can do things we think are impossible!" His eyes rested on Shaniqua sitting in the third row.

She glanced around to see if he was really looking at her. There were at least three hundred other people sitting in the pews. Why was he focusing on her? She knew she should have taken a seat in the back where all the teenagers usually sat, but Granny had asked her to sit upfront so they could pray together at the altar.

Reverend Cosby wiped his brow with his handkerchief and looked back at Shaniqua.

She squirmed in her seat, wondering if Granny had shared their family business with him. She hoped not, that would have been too embarrassing. She vowed not to tell anyone, not even her best friends.

"When times get hard and you feel you have no way out, you must have faith." Reverend Cosby pointed indirectly at Shaniqua. "You can achieve what the mind can conceive. Young people—that means whatever you think you can do, you can do! Some of us may not have the best parents, but don't let that stop you. Young people do not allow yourselves to develop negative, sinful habitual responses that can become character patterns. Do not harbor bitterness. It will gradually destroy you from within and keep you from living a full and victorious Christian life. Place the matter in God's hands, agreeing with Him that any vengeance is to be His, not yours."

The organ struck a chord, prompting the saints to respond with cries of joy.

On the way home Shaniqua thought of the sermon. Her mind raced back to her talk with Mr. Evans, his words echoing in her head. "Do better than your parents did. Make better life choices." Shaniqua looked at Granny sitting in the front seat of the church van talking with Mr. Tucker, the driver. Her mind crowded with memories-memories of the early days when she use to stick her fingers in her grandmother's mouth and Granny would pretend to bite at them without her teeth in her mouth. And Shaniqua would crack up laughing until Granny grew tired of playing. And how Granny would sit on the couch and Shaniqua would practice putting ponytails in her grandmother's hair. Granny made her feel like she would be a great hairdresser someday. Shaniqua chuckled. Barrettes looked funny on Granny.

It would break Granny's heart if she dropped out of school. She would have to come up with another plan. Granny meant more to her than she meant to herself, she thought. Everyone had disappointed Granny and she wasn't going to be the next one to let her down. Reverend Cosby and Mr. Evans were both right. At that very moment, Shaniqua decided she wasn't going to be like Karen, Nee Nee and the rest of the family. She was going to be somebody. She was going to achieve things in life. She wasn't going to be a poor adult. It was because of her mother that she lived in poverty. She was going to get a job, a respectable job that Granny could brag about to the church members. She would work, but not at the expense of quitting school. She would do both. She had to; their lives depended on it.

When they arrived home, Shaniqua immediately went to her bedroom. She took a seat on the edge of her bed staring at the dingy, thin rug and promised herself that she would one day know what it was like to step out onto a fluffy white rug. Once she became an adult, never again would she wash up with rags so thin that she could literally see through. Never again sleep with cotton stuffed in her ears for fear of roaches crawling in while she slept. One day she would leave this life behind her and take Granny with her. Though they didn't live in the Hillside Housing projects, their duplex was only a few blocks away. The projects had never been a pretty place. Nothing but dirt poor and brave souls entered the compound. There was barely a brick that didn't have some type of graffiti on it, while old bloodstains decorated the filthy, crumbling concrete. Her grandmother didn't deserve to live so close to people who could take a person's life like they were stomping on an ant.

Shaniqua dropped to her knees, kneeling as she had not knelt in awhile. Granny had taught her that the way to pray was to forget everything and everyone but Jesus; to pour out of the heart, like dirty mop water from a bucket, all evil thoughts.

The light of day was gone when Shaniqua laced up a pair of old sneakers and dashed out the door and jogged up the block to meet Nee Nee. When Shaniqua returned home, she walked into Granny's bedroom and put the money down on her high bed. Her grandmother looked up from the bible, peered over the rim of her reading glasses with the connecting tarnished chain dangling at the sides of her face. "What's this for?"

"Our rent money."

Granny removed her eyeglasses from her face. "Chile, where you get that money from?"

Shaniqua sucked on her teeth.

"Chile, you deaf?"

"No, ma'am." Shaniqua drew in a deep breath and crossed her fingers. "Brittany."

"Well, you give it back to her, hear. Church looks out after its family. Everything works together for good for them that love the Lawd."

"Yes, ma'am."

"Lawd willing, you and me gone be all right. You just worry 'bout school."

"Yes, ma'am," Shaniqua said and made her way upstairs.

She wondered if Granny suspected that she had been contemplating dropping out. Granny always said, "I know what you gone do before you do!"

Chapter 11

Monday morning, Natasha entered through the double doors of the school, her long, lean legs made confident strides alongside her brother, Nate. Natasha immediately felt the weight of staring eyes. Groups of students watched them as they passed the administrative office. Maybe they were staring at him. Or maybe they presumed she and Nate were a couple or something, but they looked too much alike to make that assumption. Both of them had tall, slender frames, the same warm brown complexion, chiseled cheekbones, and narrow eyes. What else could they be staring at? Natasha looked down to see if toilet paper was stuck to her shoe, but all she saw was the shiny coral-colored polish on her toenails. "Alright, Nate, I'm going to catch up with my man."

Nate shot her a mean look. "Look Tasha, I already told you about calling that dude your boyfriend. The only reason why guys call girls their girlfriend is because they are expecting to hit it."

"Stephen's not like that."

"Yeah, alright. You keep thinking that," Nate said,

then ventured off with his basketball teammate.

Natasha changed her mind about meeting Stephen and strolled alone to the commons area to meet her girlfriends when she caught her reflection in the glass trophy case. She smiled at herself. When she left home that morning, she thought she looked decent, even cute. Her hair was flat-ironed silky straight and kissed her shoulders. She wasn't wearing "war paint," as her dad called makeup, except for black mascara and clear lip gloss. Natasha scanned the area for Shaniqua and Brittany, but didn't see them, so she made her way through the crowded hallway down to Stephen's locker. Stephen was digging around in his locker when Natasha cupped her hands over his eyes and kissed him on the cheek. He turned around and hugged her tightly, sending chills through her body.

"How are you?" Natasha said, grinning.

She and Stephen weren't exactly the type to show affection at school. It wasn't her style. She had seen girls all hugged up with their boyfriends one week and then the next, they'd be looking long-faced when they broke up. But for some strange reason, Natasha felt like showing affection to her boyfriend, regardless of who was watching.

"Fine. Have you been to your locker yet?" Stephen asked.

"No, I need to go."

Stephen and Natasha started down the hallway when one of Natasha's classmates suddenly stopped them. "Tasha, I saw you on Saturday. Girl, you were tight to def! I didn't know you were a model," Melanie said.

Natasha nodded shyly and smiled.

"Pssst, puh-leeze. She was not all that," Natasha thought she overheard someone say. She wondered if they were talking about her. She glanced around. It was Kendra and Jasmine, two juniors who had always seemed cool.

"Hi, Stephen," Kendra, said, slow and seductive, and then both girls burst into giggles.

Natasha scrunched her head in confusion. Why hadn't they spoken to her, too? Natasha turned to Stephen who had a stupid grin on his face. She wanted to swipe it off. She wasn't a jealous person; then again she never had a boyfriend to be jealous over. And she wasn't about to get that way with Stephen. Jealousy was a negative characteristic.

Shaniqua and Brittany waited quietly at the lunch table for Natasha to join them. They were trying not to get into a fight today. Natasha greeted them as usual and took her seat.

Shaniqua toyed with her cold fries. "Hey Ms. Thang, you're the talk of the school. Everybody's talking about how you've changed since last year, how you're a big time model now."

"Big time," Natasha chuckled. "Don't think so."

"Sorry, I couldn't make it. My mom and I were doing a taste test for my birthday cake," Brittany said. "My party is going to be off the chain . . ."

Shaniqua rolled her eyes. "Well, you could have at least called."

Natasha glanced across the cafeteria and spotted Kendra and her friend staring at her. She could have sworn Kendra mouthed, "What the hell you lookin' at?" Natasha quickly put her head back down. She didn't want any trouble with this girl. Natasha hadn't known much about Kendra, except she was a junior, somewhat cute in the face with a protruding forehead and a long straight weave that ran down her back. Kendra had a honey-colored complexion and was about the same height as Brittany. Natasha wondered if she should share this with her girls, but then they would look over and that would just add fuel to the fire. Natasha sat quietly through lunch listening to Brittany pour over every detail of her party.

Natasha went through the remainder of the day hearing everything from "Congratulations," "How much money you make?" to "I want to model, too!" She had no idea the word would travel so quickly. She hated that everyone was putting her on a pedestal that she didn't deserve to be on. She was still hoping to make it in the business.

When she came around the corner on her way to art class, she saw Stephen and Kendra walking slowly, smiling and laughing. Natasha wondered what to do. There was no one to consult. She had to think fast. Walking over to them would make her look jealous, but not saying anything at all while some chick walked down the hall with her boyfriend was disrespectful. Why didn't Stephen stop her? Tell her that he already had a girl. Natasha took long strides, forgetting her new model stroll. This was no time to be cute. This chick needed to be checked and with quickness. Natasha's heart thumped in her chest as she suddenly appeared on the other side of Stephen.

He grinned. "Hey, Tasha."

"Hey," she said dryly, for lack of something more profound.

Stephen nonchalantly turned his attention back to Kendra. Natasha thought he was going to say something, but he just smiled at Kendra. Natasha was heated, heated enough for smoke to disperse from the top of her head.

Kendra gawked at Stephen before she spoke. "I've got to get to class. 'Bye Stephen," she said flirtatiously.

As soon as Kendra strolled off, purposely switching her big, curvy hips, Natasha couldn't hold it in. She didn't care if they were late to class or not. Mr. Arnold would have to understand this time. A funny feeling consumed her insides. Natasha wanted to yell, but she knew that wasn't a good way to handle things. Her parents had done that and it never worked for them, which is why they were divorced. Natasha drew in a deep breath to regain her composer. "What's up with that?"

"What?" Stephen said.

"Why is Kendra walking you to class?"

"She didn't walk me to class. We kind of bumped into each other and she just started talking to me."

"That's awfully funny, Stephen. Why would she be coming down the art corridor?"

"I don't know. Maybe she has a class over here, Tasha."

The bell summoned them both into the classroom. Natasha took her seat, still upset. She only hoped it didn't show on her face. Stephen was acting awfully naïve. Natasha wondered if he was enjoying this new attention. Freshman and sophomore years, no one paid him any attention; now all of a sudden, girls were noticing him.

Mr. Arnold began the class discussion about design composition, but Natasha couldn't understand anything he was saying. Anger was consuming her like a cancerous disease. She had to get rid of this very uncomfortable feeling. She needed to talk to someone, talk her anger away. Her eyes rested on the small yellow and black poster hanging at the front of the class. "A man paints with his brain and not with his hands," by Michelangelo. She didn't care to paint with either, but to save face, she whipped out her art supplies from her backpack and flashed a synthetic smile at Stephen.

Chapter 12

Shaniqua as sat in her last class fiddling with her fingers, waiting for the dismissal bell to ring. Her thoughts were on Jordan. She studied the clock while the global studies teacher's voice droned on and on about nothing. When the bell rang, she rushed out of the classroom and down the hall to her locker, curious to see if anything would happen after school since she had made that secret phone call on Friday. She grabbed her jacket and hurried out to the bus lineup. She saw Jordan and some boys hanging out as usual by his car. A sinking feeling crept in. Disappointed, she stepped onto the bus. Her plan had failed. Maybe the police weren't going to do anything because she neglected to leave her name and phone number.

The bus quickly filled up with rambunctious students. Shaniqua leaned her head against the glass and tuned them out. All of sudden, someone shouted, "Strike Force got Jordan and dem down on da ground!"

Shaniqua whipped her head around to look out the back window of the bus. Several officers dressed in black military fatigues had Jordan and his partners sprawled out on the ground while two other officers searched the car. "Da Black Cats got 'em, dey in trouble now!" Another voice exclaimed from the back of the bus.

The bus driver cranked the engine. Shaniqua hoped he would at least wait long enough to witness what happened. When the bus began to move, she jumped up from her seat, she needed to see what was going down. One by one, the officers clamped handcuffs on the boys, snatched them off the ground and shoved them in the back of the patrol cars. Jordan appeared to be arguing with an officer because he looked like he was yelling. The officer slammed Jordan on the hood of his car and handcuffed him. Shaniqua sat back down as the bus pulled out onto Covington highway. "You're getting written up, young lady," the bus driver yelled. Shaniqua grinned and thought it was well worth it; at least one menace to society would be no more.

Brittany hurried through the mustard-colored hallways to her first cheerleading practice after school. She changed into a maroon t-shirt and black shorts and took a seat on the gym floor next to Mina Morales, a cute Hispanic girl. Brittany offered a friendly, "Hello."

Mina smiled, her little teeth shining brightly against her dark lipstick. "Hey, how are you?" she said.

A sigh escaped Brittany's lips. "A little nervous."

"Girl, don't be. I've been on the squad since my freshman year. It's nothing to it. My name's Mina."

"I'm Brittany, nice to meet you. I've seen you before at the games."

"Oh really?" Mina said, trying to act surprised.

Mina was one of the most popular cheerleaders on the squad. One, because she was a flyer and two, she was very attractive. She had a smooth, bronze-colored complexion, a well-sculpted face and a sleek, black ponytail that hung midway down her back. Heavy mascara and liquid eyeliner accented her large dark eyes and long lashes. "I've seen you around, too. You're the rich kid."

Brittany snickered, "Not!"

"Coach mentioned something about your mom helping to buy new mats."

Brittany nodded, though she didn't know anything about it.

Mina drew her short, muscular legs to her chest, wrapped her arms around them to shield them from the cool draft. "Was that your first time trying out?"

Brittany grinned. "I couldn't try out before because I had piano practice after school and now that I'm not playing anymore, I decided to give it a try."

The varsity coach came over and instructed the girls to start their stretching routine. Brittany relaxed into the feeling of friendship, happy to have made a new friend, a popular friend.

ᘓ

When practiced ended, Brittany took Mina outside to meet her dad. Brittany swung open the car door, "Hi Daddy, this is Mina."

Mr. Brown offered a half-smile. "Nice to meet you."

Brittany waved goodbye to Mina and slid into the front seat. She turned to face her dad; his jaws were clenched. The hairs on Brittany's arms stood up. She had that sinking feeling in her stomach as if she had just swallowed a rock.

Mr. Brown spoke slow and deliberate. "Do you mind explaining how the Maxima got the dent in the driver's side door?"

Brittany swallowed so hard she wondered if her tongue was still in her mouth. If not, at least she would have an excuse for not speaking. She thought of lying her way out, but there was no one else in the house to blame. Her brother Kevin came home weekly to get his clothes washed and to rob them of groceries, but he had his own Mustang, his baby, that he loved dearly, so he hadn't driven the Maxima in years. No one had, except her.

"I'm sorry I don't hear you? What's the matter, the cat got your tongue?"

Brittany fiddled with her fingers. "No, sir."

"What happened to the Maxima?" her dad said sternly.

Too afraid to speak and too afraid not to, she shrugged her shoulders.

"Did you drive it?" His voice was razor sharp.

Her eyes followed the white lines on the black pavement. "Yeah."

"Yeah?"

"I mean, yes, sir."

"You must have asked your mom for permission because you didn't ask me."

"No, sir."

"I'm going to talk with your cheerleading coach—I don't think you can be trusted enough to do extra curricular activities right now, and you can kiss your party goodbye."

Tears streaked down Brittany's face as they rode home in silence.

Mrs. Brown greeted them at the door. Brittany silently searched her mother's eyes for help, but Mrs. Brown only offered a useless "I-know-how-you-feel look."

"Up to your room, now!" Mr. Brown's voice boomed through the house.

Brittany stomped up the stairs. She hated her parents, hated them like she hated liver and onions. How could they take cheerleading away from her just like that? For once in her life, she finally had a chance to do something that she really wanted to do. How many years had she spent playing the stupid piano for them when she wanted to cheer for little league football? Brittany peeled off her practice uniform and trampled them. She left the shorts and t-shirt lying on the floor, which was a definite no-no, but what else could they do to her that they hadn't already done. Now she had no cheerleading and no super-sixteen birthday party. Brittany buried her face in her oversized Tweety bird's soft stomach and whimpered herself to sleep.

When the sound of her parents arguing awoke her, Brittany quick tiptoed down the hall and stood outside the double doors of her parents' bedroom, eavesdropping. Her parents rarely argued. Whenever her mother became upset with her father, he would do funny things in the midst of the argument to make her laugh, like make funny faces or tickle her. They never stayed mad at one another for long. Though, Brittany could tell her dad was in no mood to diffuse the argument with humorous antics tonight.

"I don't care if you did give the school that money already. Brittany does not deserve to participate in extra curricular activities," Brittany's father said with finality.

"Oh, Albert, lighten up. Haven't you ever done anything when you were a kid that you shouldn't have?"

"Yes, and I ended up behind bars. Is that what you want for our kids, to come up the same way I did?"

Brittany's mouth dropped. She knew her dad had been locked up before, but he never told her what he had done. She hoped her mother would get it out of him tonight; she desperately wanted to know.

"Albert, I think you're being much too hard on the

child. It's not like she stole the neighbor's car."

"That's not the point."

"I think if we take cheerleading away from her, we'll be sorry; she's going to rebel."

"She's not going to rebel in my house!"

"Okay, please, baby, do it for me." Mrs. Brown's voice broke into a soft, pleading cadence. "Let our only daughter stay on the squad, please."

There was a long silence and then a burst of high-pitched giggles that meant her father was probably tickling her mother. Brittany tiptoed back down the hall to her bedroom, elated that her mom had won. She loved her mother and wouldn't change her for the world.

Chapter 13

The next morning, Brittany kissed her dad's cheek, and then gracefully stepped out of his silver Mercedes. She carefully positioned her new pink Gucci bag over her shoulder and slid strands of her long mane behind her ear, then smiled sweetly at her dad, letting her dimples do all the charming. "Daddy, that's the car I want for my sweet sixteen," she said, pointing to the white Lexus coupe in front of their car before closing the car door. She could tell he was considering it.

Mr. Brown rolled down the car window. "As far as I'm concerned, you're not having a party. Now, have a good day."

Brittany rolled her eyes and stormed away. She thought her parents had settled that last night. How could he do that to her? She had been planning for this party for years. She caught up with Natasha and Shaniqua in the commons area. "Y'all are not going to believe this," Brittany said.

"What?" both girls said in unison.

"My dad's not letting me have my party."

Shaniqua sniggered.

"Shut up, Shaniqua. It's not funny."

"What happened?" Natasha asked.

"He found out about the car wreck I had in the Maxima."

Shaniqua chuckled. "Duhhh! Brittany, we told you that was going to happen. You should have listened to us. But no, Ms. Know-it-all thinks she knows everything. You don't have anybody to blame but yourself for that one."

"Shaniqua chill." Natasha said.

"I'm out. I'm going to homeroom."

"I heard about Jordan Kelley." Brittany sniggered. "Are you going to bail him out?"

"What? I told y'all I wasn't thinking about his cockroach-looking self. I can't stand him."

"Well, you had us worried. Didn't she Tasha, talking about how cute he looked. I hope they throw him under the jail."

"Me, too! I'm just glad I don't have to look at his prune-looking face in homeroom anymore. Alright, I'm out like gout!"

Brittany and Shaniqua started walking to their lockers. "Girl, how am I going to get my parents to agree to my party?"

Natasha shrugged.

"I have to come up with something."

That afternoon, Mr. Brown picked up Brittany from cheerleading practice. The car was intensely quiet. Mr. Brown turned on the radio. The classical music amplified the tension in the air. It resembled the music in a scary movie when a victim was being extinguished. Brittany stared listlessly out the car window trying to come up with something, anything that would help change her dad's mind. "Dad, I want to apologize."

Mr. Brown remained quiet.

Brittany bit her bottom lip. This was going to be a lot harder than she anticipated, not a quick, easy fix like previous times. She had to find some way to touch his heart. "I know taking the car was wrong. I'm very ashamed of my actions. You and mom work so hard to give me everything. You're right. I don't deserve to have the party. I want you to take the money out of my savings account and have the door repaired. If that's not enough, I'll get a job to help pay for it. I just don't want you to be mad at me anymore."

"I'm not mad, just disappointed."

Tears surfaced in Brittany's eyes. "I promise, I will never do it again."

"Uh huh," Mr. Brown said and kept his focus on the road.

Brittany sank in her seat. Her heart was heavy, her mind clouded. Her heartfelt plea had been ignored. It was useless. There was no way to undo the damage. She had tried and failed.

Chapter 14

Friday night, Brittany studied her thighs in the framed, oval shaped cheval mirror in her bedroom, looking for signs of cellulite. As one of the heaviest cheerleaders on the squad, the last thing she needed people to see was additional evidence of her plumpness. When she finished dressing in her cheerleading uniform, she pranced around in the mirror, dancing, doing silly movements that she would never do in public. Finally, she would have her chance to cheer at the school's first football game of the season. She was tying a maroon ribbon around her ponytail when she heard a knock at the door. "Come in."

"Hey babe, ahhhh, don't you look precious. I think I'm going to cry."

"Mom, get a grip. It's not that serious."

"I just never thought that you would want to do something that I did. I never thought I would be old enough to have a child in high school."

"What about Kevin? Hello?"

"I mean a cheerleader." Mrs. Brown placed her hand across her forehead. "Sorry, I'm having a moment. I wish your dad were here to see you."

"I don't. He'd probably change his mind about letting me go."

"No, he's proud of you, too. He just wants you to not act deceitful."

Brittany rolled her eyes without her mom noticing. "Mom, you have to beg him to let me have my party. Please, Mommy, we've been planning it for years!"

"Brittany Ann, I told you already, I'm working on it. Now just give your dad some time. Oh, I wish he were here to see you."

Brittany smirked. "Take a picture."

"You're right. Stay there. I'll be right back." Mrs. Brown went flying out of the bedroom.

"Mom, I was kidding!" Brittany yelled after her.

Mrs. Brown came back in a flash and posted Brittany up against her lavender flowered print wallpaper. This reminded Brittany of when she first began playing the piano and her mom took photos of her playing, then sent them out to all the family. Brittany smiled through gritted teeth, thinking there is such a thing as overdoing it. Granted, she was very excited to be a cheerleader, but her mom was taking it to the extreme. "Mom, I have to go. I can't be late."

"Okay, babe, let me put on my sweatshirt. I'm so excited to see my baby cheer for the first time."

Brittany's eyes grew large as two official size baseballs. "You're kidding! Please tell me you're not coming into the game."

"Yes, why, is it a problem? I want to see my baby cheer."

Brittany huffed. “Okay, fine. Come in, but Mom, you have to promise me you’ll leave at half time.”

Mrs. Brown looked confused. “So you want me to go all the way back home and then come back to pick you up after the game?”

Brittany decided that this was the perfect opportunity to tell her mom about going out to eat with the squad after the game. On the other hand, if her mother saw the coach, she would surely say something. Time was ticking. Brittany pulled an old trick out the bag. Whining always worked. She touched her mother shoulders. “Please, Mommy, just this once, leave at half time, I’ll even give you gas money out of my allowance, pretty please.”

“Fine, Brittany Ann.”

The bright lights illuminated the stadium while the visiting team was on the field stretching. Both sides of the stands were filled to capacity with fans singing and dancing along to Miller Grove’s band rendition of a hip-hop song. Brittany took her place next to Mina on the front line. Nervous energy coursed through her because after tonight everyone would know her and not just as the-girl-who-was-riding-in-the-car-with-Jared-the-night-he-died, but as a varsity cheerleader. Brittany offered the crowd a wide smile to show off her bright, white teeth, and then tugged at the bottom of her skirt in the back. She knew her derriere was rounder and plumper than the other girls, so it was a necessity to keep her skirt from rising. Silently, she prayed that she didn't look like a fat cheerleader. Nobody wanted to be known as the fat cheerleader. To be a fat cheerleader was like not being a cheerleader at all. Everyone ignored you.

At half time, Brittany watched her mom leave the stands as promised. Brittany decided to give her a few minutes to make it to the car before she telephoned her. "Mom, Coach Felder is taking the squad out after the game. She said she would bring me home. Can I go?"

"Alright. I don't know what your dad'll say, so don't stay out too late. Ten-thirty, Brittany Ann."

"Thanks Mom, love you!" Brittany said. She and Mina slapped high fives.

Mina smiled. "Chica, I can't wait for you to meet Marcus, he's fine, not finer than my man, but he's a hotty, Dotty, with a hotty body!"

They both laughed.

Brittany thought she heard someone call her name. She searched the crowd and saw Natasha and Shaniqua standing at the fence. She gently swayed her hips as she made her way over to them with Mina trailing behind. Brittany tugged at her skirt and sucked in her stomach as she stood in front of her friends. "Hey y'all. What's up? How am I doing out there?"

Mina interjected. "I told her she didn't have anything to worry about."

Shaniqua shot Mina a look that could have

decapitated her had her eyes been two knives and then smiled at Brittany. "You straight, girl."

"Yeah, you look awesome, Brit," Natasha added.

Brittany offered an electric smile, then tugged at the bottom of her skirt in the back. "Thanks guys. So what are y'all doing after the game?"

Natasha and Shaniqua gave each other curious looks. "Why are you asking? Are your parents letting you hang out or something?"

"Yep! Mina and I are going to meet up with some friends of hers."

Shaniqua folded her arms across her chest and offered Natasha an I-told-you-so look.

"That's cool, your parents are letting you hang out. We're just going to get a bite to eat," Natasha said.

"Have fun! We have to get back. See ya!" Brittany said, and bounced away in the infamous peppy, cheerleading manner.

Mina led the way across the field. "Why were your girls looking at me like they don't like me or something?"

"Oh, you must be talking about Shaniqua. She's probably jealous because she didn't make the squad. Don't worry about her."

Brittany and Mina parked in the lot of the pizza parlor

that everyone frequented after games. Brittany checked herself in the mirror, offering an unsure smile. Mina advised her to bring a change of clothes, but Brittany told her she wouldn't be able to sneak a change of clothes out of the house. Brittany knew all she had to do was stuff them in her oversized Louis Vuitton bag and her mother would have never questioned her about it. Truth is she wanted to meet Marcus wearing her cheerleading uniform. She hoped he was as cute as Mina had described.

Marcus was a defensive tackle for Stephen High and a lot of girls liked him. She only hoped he wouldn't think she was a fat cheerleader. Brittany reached in the back seat to grab her jacket, just in case she needed a cover up. Then she untied the ribbon in her hair, releasing her soft curls to dangle playfully around her shoulders. Her hair was the perfect distraction. As her mother always said, "Accentuate the positive. Hair is to head, what teeth are to mouth." Her hair was her crowning glory, silky jet black with long layers. Brittany worked hard to keep it healthy with weekly visits to the hair salon and wrapping it nightly in silk sleep caps. She had been accused countless times of wearing weave—the good kind like Janet Jackson. Some boy would always try to feel around in her head for tracks and she'd swat his hand away.

Brittany used the visor mirror to add an extra coat of lip shine, hoping it didn't look like she'd been greasin' on fried chicken," a phrase her mother used to describe grossly shiny lips.

"Chica, come on, before they leave us," Mina said, closing the car door.

Brittany stepped out of the car, one pointy foot at a time, using her ballet skills from years ago. She sashayed her curvy hips across the parking lot just in case the boys were watching from inside. She didn't let her mother know, but she watched everything she did. When she was a little girl, her mom seemed dumb for displaying those crazy antics, but now that Brittany was approaching womanhood, she understood her mother better. Her mom knew how to charm and had the wits and guts to do anything. Mrs. Brown always boasted about snagging Brittany's dad from another girl in college.

Mina led the way into the restaurant and greeted her boyfriend Carlos with a juicy kiss on the lips. Mina turned to Marcus. "Marcus, meet my girl, Brittany."

Brittany parted her lips into a soft smile, letting her dimples do all the charming. She flung her hair behind her ear and reached out to shake Marcus's hand. "Hello."

Marcus stood up and shook Brittany's hand. "How are you?"

He was just a few inches taller than Brittany, which put him at average height for a male. His voice was deep. Brittany hadn't known any boys at her school with a voice as deep as his. She wondered if he really was in high school or college. "Nice to meet you, Marcus."

Mina interrupted, "And this is my man, Carlos."

Carlos continued sitting and eating his pizza. "What's up? Eh, Mina go tell the waitress to bring me another cherry lemonade."

"Carlos, I'm sure she's coming back to the table," Mina said.

"I ain't waiting, so go tell her what I said."

"Papi!" she said, her voice cloaked in embarrassment.

Mina locked eyes with Brittany before leaving the table.

Marcus stepped aside. "Brittany, please, have a seat here. I promise I don't bite . . . at least most times."

His lips parted into a soft smile, captivating Brittany. She had a thing for teeth. After all the money her parents had spent straightening her teeth, there was no way she was going to settle for a snaggletooth-Tony. Either Marcus was really blessed or his parents spent goo-gobs on his mouth, too. "Thanks," she said, sliding into the booth.

Their attraction was instant. Brittany couldn't stop smiling and neither could Marcus. He was so cute. His skin was football brown and smooth. She wanted to reach out and touch it. His eyelashes were long and thick, drawing attention to his intense dark brown eyes.

Out of habit, Brittany glanced down at her perfectly manicured nails to make sure she hadn't chipped any nails during the game, even though she kept them short. Her eyes traveled up her left arm to her diamond encrusted pink watch. The time read 10:15 p.m. Panic set in. She only had fifteen minutes before she was supposed to be home. It would take her at least that long to get home if they left now. What was she going to do? She could call her mom and tell her that all the girls hadn't finished eating, but then her dad would offer to come get her, so that wouldn't work. Anxiety ran through her, Brittany became rigid. Her shoulders stiffened, her legs locked in place. She held her hands just in case they decided to shake. When Mina returned to the table,

Brittany tried eyeing Mina to let her know that it was time to go, but Mina was still too embarrassed to make eye contact.

Marcus studied Brittany. "So, what's up with you?"

Brittany offered a goofy grin. "Nothing. What's up with you?"

Marcus relaxed in the seat. "I'm chillin'. So what do you want to get into tonight?"

Brittany wanted to tell him, "This is it, sitting in the pizza parlor with you," but she refrained.

Marcus grinned. "Well, you want to go for a ride or something? Carlos can ride with Mina and I'll take you home."

Brittany studied their half-eaten pepperoni pizza, trying to process it all. Time was ticking too freakin' fast. In five minutes, she was supposed to be home. She looked to Mina for the answer.

Mina nodded. "It's cool. Marcus is a good guy." Mina looked back at Carlos who was busy flirting with another girl across the room. "What are you doing?"

Carlos scrunched his face so tightly it resembled a chipmunk's. "What do you mean, what am I doing?"

Mina sucked on her teeth. "Nothing, Carlos, nothing."

"Damn right."

Marcus touched Brittany's arm, sending chills up to her mouth, freezing her speech. "Brittany, let's go."

Brittany stood up and looked at Mina who had tears welling up in her eyes. Brittany didn't know what to do. "Are you okay?"

Mina nodded. "See you later."

Marcus dapped Carlos goodbye and they walked to

Marcus's truck, a dusty blue Blazer.

Brittany slid her hair behind her ear, this time from nervousness. "So, umm, are they okay?"

Marcus opened the car door for Brittany, "They're always like that."

"Ueww!"

Marcus chuckled. "So where do you want to go?"

Brittany looked at her watch—it was now 10:30 p.m.—she was definitely going to be late. She thought about her sweet sixteen party, her Lexus, and Marcus. Her mind was running rampant. She had to think of a quick lie. There was no way she was going to tell Marcus that she had a ten-thirty curfew. Brittany reached in her purse for her vibrating cell phone; her parents had called two minutes earlier.

"Hey, I should get home. My dad's out of town and my mom is sick. I promised her I wouldn't be out late."

"Oh, that's cool. No problem."

A wave of relief washed over Brittany's face, resulting in a smile. Marcus was cool.

When they arrived, the porch and chandelier lights were on, which meant someone was still up. Brittany's heart pounded so hard in her chest she wondered if Marcus could hear it.

"Your crib is tight."

"Wait, wait!" Brittany yelled. "Don't turn into my driveway."

Marcus hit the brakes.

"I don't want the loud motor to wake my parents, I mean my mom, if she's sleeping."

"Cool. So can I have your number?" Marcus asked.

"I'll get yours from Mina. I've got to go. You don't have to wait for me," Brittany said and bailed out of the truck, running down the long driveway. There was no way she was going to the front door so that her parents could look out and see Marcus's truck. She had to get in the house another way. She zipped around to the back patio door and turned the handle. It was locked. Sweat beaded down the sides of her face causing loose strands of her hair to stick. Brittany glanced at the pool glistening under the quarter moon in the starry night sky. Her eyes scanned the area and rested on the pool entrance into the house. She crossed her fingers, said a hope-to-God prayer and darted over to the door. She twisted the knob gently and the latch unlocked. "Thank God," she whispered and tiptoed in quietly to the back stairwell.

"Brittany!" her dad called out. His heavy voice resonated throughout the first level of the house.

She froze with her right foot planted on the first step, and turned around slowly.

Dressed in the black silk pajamas she had given him for Father's Day the year before, he quickly made his way to her. His round rim reading glasses sat crookedly on his face, a medical journal was clutched tightly underneath his armpit. "What time is it, young lady?"

Brittany wanted to lie and say that she didn't have her watch on, but tiny diamonds were sparkling underneath the recessed light. "Ten fifty-five."

"And what time is curfew?"

"Ten-thirty," Brittany muttered.

"Speak up, we don't mumble in this house. What time is curfew?"

"Ten-thirty. But Daddy, it wasn't my fault. Coach Felder had to drop off one of the other girls. I asked her to drop me off first, but she said that it was out of her way to do that."

Mr. Brown nodded slowly in defeat.

Brittany fought back her smile, because it would signify that she had won. "Daddy, why can't I stay out later like everybody else?"

"Because you're not like everybody else. If everyone jumps off a cliff, are you going to do it too?"

She hated when he talked like that. Why couldn't he just be normal like everybody else? "Where's Mom?"

"Asleep. Now, go to bed."

Anger set in as Brittany stalked up the stairs. Why did he feel the need to tell her to go to bed like she was still ten years old? Why couldn't she go when she grew tired like everybody else? Yet her parents had the nerve to wonder why she didn't invite friends for a sleepover. Her parents were really beginning to irk the crap out of her. She couldn't wait to go off to college and get from under their control. *Just another year and a half.*

Chapter 15

Monday morning, Brittany hurried to the commons area before going to her locker to catch up with Shaniqua and Natasha since she hadn't talked to them in two days. The commons area was noisy with laughter and loud voices from the same groups in their usual places. Brittany didn't see her friends. Normally, Shaniqua was the first one there. Brittany decided to wait on them. After a couple of minutes passed, she gave up and headed to her locker. As soon as she turned the corner to go down the B hallway, she spotted them at Natasha's locker. "Hey ladies," Brittany said. "Have I got an earful for y'all!"

Natasha offered a weak hello while Shaniqua waited to hear.

Brittany spotted Mina and waved her over to the group. Mina kept her head slightly bent as if she was trying to hide a hickey from her parents. Brittany gasped. "Oh-my-God, what happened to you?"

Mina looked up, her eyes wide with humiliation. "Nothing, I'll tell you later, I have to get to class," she said, and hurried down the hallway.

Shaniqua leaned in close to her friends. "Did y'all see that bruise on her cheek?"

"No, I was searching my locker for my French book, I can't find it." Natasha said.

"Girl, that thing was as big as my fist and purple black." Shaniqua placed her hand over her heart. "No lie, I swear to God, well, not to God, but you know what I mean."

Brittany's mind raced back to Friday night at the restaurant. Mina wore the same expression of embarrassment when she and Carlos had gotten into an argument.

Shaniqua cackled. "It looked like somebody got knocked the bleep out!"

"Shaniqua, shut up! There you go, starting rumors," Brittany retorted.

"You shut up. I'm not starting no rumors. I'm just calling it like I see it! Somebody tagged yo' girl's, Ms. Superfly Cheerleader, head!"

"You're just saying that because you're jealous that you didn't make the squad."

"Brittany, please, you can't even do a cartwheel! Your parents probably bought your way on!" Shaniqua retorted.

"Alright y'all, just chill." Natasha interrupted.
"Brittany, why don't you try to talk to Mina, find out what happened."

Brittany shifted her book bag on her back. "I'll try to catch up with her at lunch."

Shaniqua smirked. "Yeah, you always running up behind her!"

"Brittany glared at Shaniqua. "What?"

The bell refereed and the girls scattered to class.

Huffing mad, Brittany entered homeroom without acknowledging her teacher, Ms. Mathis. Shaniqua was being a pain in the butt. It wasn't like it was her fault that she didn't make the squad. She told her not to wear those booty shorts to the tryouts. Nor was it her fault that folks still remembered what happened last year and was still referring to her as a "ho-cake." A part of Brittany wanted to end the friendship with Shaniqua, but how could she—it had always been the three of them since freshman year. Still hot, she claimed her seat and began doodling on her chemistry notebook. She wrote: Brittany, Natasha, Mina, and Shaniqua, then, drew a big, bold X over Shaniqua's name.

It was lunchtime, and Brittany had promised herself she was going to ignore Shaniqua's ignorance. As her mom always instructed, "When someone's acting ignorant, don't get down on their level, raise them to yours and if you can't do that, ignore them." Brittany sat her tray down, her mother's advice echoing in her head.

"Hey girl," Natasha said.

"What's the matter, can't find your new best buddy?" Shaniqua mimicked.

"As a matter of fact, she doesn't have this lunch period. And you would have known that if you hadn't jumped down my throat this morning." Brittany said, then bit into the greasy cheese pizza. Mrs. Brown's words of advice were disappearing fast. Brittany mustered a fake smile at Shaniqua. She swallowed her food and then began speaking softly. "Y'all will never guess what happened to me on Friday night? I met the finest boy. His name is Marcus Graham. He's a senior at Stephen High. And he's a football player, I might add."

"Really, Brit?" Natasha asked. "How did you guys meet?"

"Mina intro . . ."

"Of course," Shaniqua interrupted.

"Don't hate, just because he's not a loser like Jordan."

"See, why'd you have to go there?" Shaniqua said. "Well, I hope you don't get played."

"Oh, me, babygirl, that will never be!" Brittany chimed. "I'm not a sucker."

"So what are you trying to say, Brittany, I'm a sucka?"

"Did I say you were?"

"Both of y'all just stop, please," Natasha pleaded. "Every time we get together, y'all are fighting. I can't deal with this. It's not fun, it's miserable."

"Tell it to Shaniqua," Brittany added.

"Tell it to yo' momma!" Shaniqua scoffed.

Natasha grabbed her tray and stormed off. Shaniqua followed, while Brittany sat there trying to finish her lunch. She was angry, but anger never dissolved her appetite like it did other people's. Shaniqua had succeeded, she pulled the ugly out of her.

Mina was bent down tying her shoelaces when Brittany arrived for cheerleading practice. When Mina stood up to stretch, Brittany zeroed in on the large, dark discoloration on her cheek. "So what did you and Carlos do after we left Friday night?"

Mina shook her head.

"Well, what did y'all do?"

"Nothing," Mina responded dryly.

"What happened to your face?"

"Nothing. I don't want to talk about it, okay?"

"Fine."

After a moment of silence, Mina turned to face Brittany. "I'm sorry. I didn't mean to ... it's just."

Brittany wrapped her arm around Mina's shoulders. "It's okay. You can trust me, let's go to the bathroom."

They made their way into the bathroom. Mina was sniffling when Brittany handed her some toilet paper.

"Did Carlos hit you?"

A long, uncomfortable silence lingered in the air, along with the stench of urine. Mina offered a slow nod.

"Why'd he do that?"

Mina shook her head. "It's my fault."

"Did you hit him first or something?"

"No."

"Then how's it your fault?"

Mina shrugged. "It's not as bad as it looks. Carlos really does love me."

"Mina, you need to leave him alone. That's crazy, that ain't love. No one has the right to put their hands on you, and especially a male. You don't have to put up with that from Carlos or anyone else. That's not love."

"Look, you don't know Carlos like I do. We've been together since I was a freshman. I know him and I know he loves me. So just butt out, okay?" Mina stormed out of the bathroom, Brittany followed. When they made it back to practice, Coach Felder had all the girls doing stretching exercises.

When practice was over, Mina offered a phony grin like it hurt to smile. "So, what do you think of Marcus?"

"I like him. I want to invite him to my birthday party . . . if I have a party," Brittany said, putting on her sweatpants. "I told him I would get his number from you. I tried calling you all weekend, but your cell wasn't on. Do you have his number with you?"

Mina jotted the number down. "Keep that conversation between us, okay?" She said, her eyes were full of sadness.

"Sure."

URBAN GODDESS

Brittany lay in bed, talking to Marcus on the phone. She discovered they had a lot in common. He wanted to go to Morehouse College and Brittany wanted to attend Spellman. Marcus was going to pledge Alpha Phi Alpha and she was going to pledge the sister sorority, Alpha Kappa Alpha. Then they could walk around the campus hand in hand, he would sport his black and gold line jacket, and she would wear her pink and green one. And everyone would tell them that they were the perfect cute couple, just like her parents had been in college. Brittany smiled at the thought.

Chapter 16

Saturday afternoon, Natasha relaxed beside Stephen on her dad's black leather sofa, the glow of affection lighting her face. She was glad that her brothers and dad had gone to Neil's football game. Natasha flicked on her dad's new, wall-mounted, flat screen plasma TV. It changed the whole look of the family room, giving it a more contemporary, cosmopolitan look. Her dad's house wasn't the most decorative. Very few pictures graced the walls. There were no curtains hanging; only dusty white faux wood blinds.

"So, what do you want to watch?" Natasha asked, using the remote control to channel surf.

"You," Stephen said.

Her eyes bucked. Stephen had not only changed physically over the summer, but he was acting different, cooler. She wondered if his new look had gone to his head or if that girl, Kendra, chasing him was giving him a big head.

Stephen scooted closer and wrapped his arm around her shoulder.

She flicked the channels faster. Sweat pressed through the pores in Natasha's forehead. She wanted to wipe it, but that would make her look goofier. Her thoughts raced back to her and Nate's conversation.

Stephen gently removed the remote from her hand and set it on an end table.

Natasha jumped up. "Uh, I've got to turn off the oven. I'll be right back," she said without waiting for a response. She scurried into the half bathroom on the first floor. Her face was gross with sweat. Her modeling instructor would have had a fit. Natasha carefully dabbed it dry with toilet paper. She wondered if Stephen was trying to get busy. She liked him, but if need be, she could let him go in an instant. Their relationship was not that serious, she told herself. How dare he put pressure on her that way? Maybe Nate was right afterall. Stephen was supposed to be different, not like the others—only after one thing. A mean look came over her. She had to give him a piece of her mind. He could take his yellow banana-looking butt on—on to Kendra. Natasha swung open the bathroom door with a vengeance, marched into the family room, forgetting her new model walk, looked at Stephen who was sitting on the couch, laughing at the Justice League cartoons. She plopped down on the sofa at the other end.

"What's wrong with you?" Stephen said.

Natasha's arms were tucked firmly across her chest. "I don't like where this relationship is headed."

"What do you mean? I thought we got past Kendra."

"That's not what I'm talking about."

She met his eyes and for a long moment, he simply stared at her, confused.

Natasha repositioned her legs underneath her bottom and clasped her hands in her lap. "Stephen, I'm not trying to get busy with you now!" she blurted out.

Stephen's eyebrows gathered in the center of his forehead and then he dropped his gaze to the floor. "I'm not trying to get busy with you either."

"Then why were you just coming at me like that?"

"I'm sorry you thought that." Stephen's voice softened, "Tasha, I really like you. You're a very special girl and I don't want to do anything to mess up our relationship. Plus, I'm not ready to go down that road either."

Natasha giggled. "You're a virgin?"

Stephen hesitated. His focus fell into his lap. A lot was riding on his answer. Cool guys weren't supposed to be virgins. Only the nerds. Still, silence loomed. The only noise was Superman shouting, "We must catch them!" blaring from the surround sound speakers in the ceiling.

"Stephen, if you are, it's okay. I am, too. And I'm proud to still be one."

He offered a slow nod.

Natasha slid closer to Stephen. "Cool. We're on the same page."

She intertwined her fingers through his, rested her head on his shoulder and kissed him softly on his neck. Stephen responded by repositioning her in his arms. Natasha relaxed in his warm cradle. Her eyes were next to his Adam's apple. He moistened his lips with his tongue in a very sensual way and leaned down to place a gentle kiss on her forehead and another on her lips.

Natasha parted her lips and let her tongue meet his. She could feel the intensity of his heartbeat through the palm of his hand. They kissed until their lips grew numb.

Chapter 17

Brittany's dad had finally conceded to her super sixteenth birthday party. For weeks, the party was the talk of the school. All the cool upperclassmen had received invitations. Everyone was discussing who was going with whom and what he or she would be wearing. Girls were purchasing fancy dresses as if it were the prom. The word around the school was that Brittany would be getting the top of the line Lexus. Even seniors were planning to attend the party.

The morning of Brittany's birthday, she awoke feeling energetic. She stepped out of the bed and into her Tweety bird slippers. Nothing in the world was better than turning sixteen and inviting five hundred of your closest friends to witness it. She quickly showered and dressed as usual for her Saturday morning hair appointment, though today's appointment would be different. She would choose her own hairstyle, instead of her mother choosing. Brittany grabbed the magazine page that she ripped out from Black Hair magazine, and folded down to fit neatly in her purse.

She descended the winding staircase until she reached the bottom where a large extravagant arrangement of flowers sat on the marble table in the foyer. The colors were vibrant in purple, orange, and yellow. The card read, "Happy Sweet Sixteenth Birthday, Brittany." She inhaled their exotic scent; she would have preferred her favorite, long stemmed pink roses.

Brittany eased into the kitchen where her mother was sitting at the table eating strawberry yogurt. Mrs. Brown looked up and held her arms open. "Oh, good morning, baby. Happy Birthday!"

Brittany's lips curled into a slight smile, hiding the disappointment of not seeing her entire family waiting for her at breakfast. "Thanks."

"Grab something light and quick. We're meeting Daddy and Kevin at the Ritz for brunch after our hair appointment."

Brittany's eyes gave way to her excitement. The Ritz-Carlton on Peachtree Street was one of her favorite restaurants. They had the best Sunday brunch in town. She only hoped Saturday would be as good. It was going to be a struggle to refrain from eating a lot. She couldn't have her stomach bulging in her dress.

All day Brittany enjoyed her sixteenth birthday. From the

elaborate family brunch at the Ritz-Carlton to the lovely bottle of perfume her mother had given her. Brittany had been asking for this perfume for the past few Christmases, birthdays, and every other special occasion. She even tried to convince her mother to buy it for herself—that way Brittany could sneak and wear it. She always wanted to smell of Fleur de Lis. It was recognized as the world's most expensive perfume. When Mrs. Brown handed Brittany the lavender box over brunch, Brittany didn't get excited because she figured it was just another piece of crystal to add to her armoire. She unwrapped the package while talking with her brother, Kevin. Brittany stopped mid-sentence when her eyes fell on the tiny, handmade crystal bottle adorned with a sparkling brilliant-cut white diamond. An 18-karat gold fleur de lis decorated the front of the bottle. Brittany thought she was going to die. She reached over and hugged her mother tightly. She immediately inhaled the scent. It smelled of jasmine with a hint of balsam. She loved it. The only thing that could top that present was her new Lexus, and she couldn't wait.

Chapter 18

Natasha dusted her face with translucent powder to set her makeup. Listening to the music blaring from her Ipod, she wondered if Stephen could dance. He never went to the school dances. Maybe he'd have some hot moves to compliment his new look, she thought as she closed her bedroom door to wait for him downstairs. She was thankful that she convinced him to go. For once, she could go to a function and not have to dance in a group of girls or stand around waiting for someone to ask her. She had her own man and could pull him onto the dance floor in a moment's notice. There were some nice perks to having a boyfriend. Contrary to what Nate believed about boyfriends and girlfriends, she could relax; she had already had that talk with Stephen.

Natasha descended the stairs slowly in a strapless apple green dress, layers of soft chiffon floated behind her. Her mother and brothers were lined neatly along the bottom of the stairs. She felt like Cinderella. Ms. Harris beamed with mother's pride. "You look so beautiful."

Neil, Natasha's younger brother chuckled. "Too much

makeup!"

Nate's eyes were fixed on Stephen standing by the front door.

Ms. Harris turned to Stephen. "Alright, you take care of my sweet pea!"

Natasha wanted to die right there in the foyer. How could her mom call her that in front of him? She looked at her mother pleadingly.

Ms. Harris smiled. "Well, you do look like my little sweet pea in all that green."

Natasha shot Stephen an expression that said what her mouth would not, "Let's go!" She grabbed the shawl that she borrowed from her mother and started out the door. Once they were safely tucked away in the car, she took a moment to observe Stephen. His twists were freshly done. It made her smile that he would go through the extra trouble to get his hair done for the occasion. He was nicely clad in a black suit with a pale yellow shirt and a matching tie.

"Tasha, you look beautiful."

"Thank you," she said, grateful that it was dark so he couldn't see her blushing. "You're not too bad yourself!"

"Oh gee, thanks."

Natasha pulled the visor mirror down to check her makeup one last time. She was definitely obsessed with the mirror. She could hardly pass something without looking for her reflection. She found it in the toaster, car windows, glass doors, anything that reflected would do.

"Can I get a kiss hello?"

"No! Number one, you're driving and two, I just put on my lips."

URBAN GODDESS

All day Shaniqua sat on the tattered sofa, biting her nails, watching her grandmother sew using the old Singer machine in the living room. The machine was probably made before Granny was born. There was no way a hot-looking dress could be made using it. The wooden table was chipped in just about every imaginable spot. She hoped Granny wasn't destroying the beautiful fabric. Shaniqua loved her new fabric, a gift from a church member. Ms. Dorothy Mae owned a fabric store in downtown Stone Mountain and told Granny to bring her grandbaby and she could have her choice of fabric. When Shaniqua arrived at the store, her eyes immediately went to a beautiful, soft peach chiffon fabric, one of the most expensive fabrics there.

Now Shaniqua was sitting with her fingers crossed, praying that her grandmother didn't ruin her dress trying to add the finishes touches. Granny had been known to mess up a time or two. Like the time she made her kindergarten graduation dress with one sleeve three inches longer than the other. And all Granny said was, "Chile, who can tell, folks ain't gonna pay you no mind." But the kids noticed. Kids always notice.

Shaniqua had already decided if her dress looked homemade, she wasn't going to the party. She had it all worked out. She would try on the dress, praise Granny for a wonderful job, and then tell her that she wasn't feeling well so that her feelings wouldn't be hurt. Playing sick worked for just about every occasion except missing church. Shaniqua watched Granny's arthritic fingers hard at work. This was the absolute last outfit that Granny would ever have to make for her, she promised herself. She was getting a job. *No more homemade clothes!*

When Granny finished, Shaniqua slipped on the dress. It was a perfect fit. She admired herself in the half-cracked mirror. She had to admit that Granny didn't do so bad a job this time. Perhaps her skills had improved over the years. Shaniqua only hoped that Granny didn't think she was going to make her prom dress, too. *Absolutely not!* Granny's feelings would just have to get hurt. To be on the safe side, she was going to get a job and start saving money immediately. The junior prom was only a few months away. But for tonight, the homemade dress worked. Granny did a nice job, especially since she didn't have to bother with sleeves. Shaniqua looked gorgeous in the rhinestone strapped, tea length dress. Peach looked good on her, she thought twirling around.

Shaniqua clutched her silver handbag underneath her armpit and stepped into Nee Nee's silver stilettos, then made her way downstairs to wait for her cousin. She could have ridden with Brittany in the limo, but since Natasha wasn't riding, there was no way she was going to be sandwiched between Brittany and her new best friend, Mina. And she didn't want to feel like a third wheel by tagging alongside Natasha and Stephen.

Granny wobbled into the living room. "Chile, you sho' look purty! How you like yo' dress? Nice fit, ain't it?"

Shaniqua struck a pose with her hands on her petite hips. "I love it!"

Granny looked down at her hands. "These ole hands of mine ain't so bad after all. I told you, yo' dress would be just fine. Chile, I was sewing my own clothes when I wasn't but knee-high to a grasshopper."

She kissed her grandmother's forehead. "Alright, Granny, I think I hear Nee Nee pulling up. Love ya! Bye!"

Chapter 19

Sheathed in a navy blue, empire-waist gown with a long train, Brittany looked elegant and glamorous. A dazzling crystal band under the bust line of her dress complemented the substantial diamond necklace and earrings that she borrowed from her mother. Her stylist had swept her hair into a sexy updo. ZiZi, her mom's makeup artist had done her makeup. A smoky gray color graced her eyelids, making her appear more womanly. Three varying shades of color were on her lips, with just a touch of shine to make them look even more enticing. It wasn't often that she got to wear makeup, especially with her parents' consent, so she was going to enjoy it.

When Brittany finished running down her mental checklist, she went downstairs to inspect her wardrobe changes for the fifth time. She paced back and forth in the white formal living room waiting for the limousine to arrive with Mina. She wished her other friends could join them, but she couldn't blame Natasha for wanting to ride with Stephen. After all, she wished Marcus could ride with them, but her parents didn't know Marcus and would have never approved of it.

The black super-stretch Hummer moved slowly down the driveway, stopping in front of the door where Mrs. Brown was waiting. Brittany's dad was already at the Georgian Terrace Hotel making sure everything was in place. Brittany made her way into the foyer. She was so excited. This was the beginning of the night for her. Everything was moving along perfectly as planned. She looked at her diamond-encrusted watch—in just a few hours she would have her new Lexus. She wondered what color her parents had chosen. "Mom, please don't forget my wardrobe changes. They're over on the couch."

"Yes, Brittany, where they've been for the past few days. I won't forget. Now, go get in the car and I'll meet you at the hotel."

The chauffeur stood at the limo door waiting. Brittany was excited to ride, though it wasn't her first time. She had been in countless limos, but never without her parents, and never in a Hummer. Whenever the family traveled on business with their dad, usually to a heart surgeon conference, they usually rode in a typical, boring black limo from the airport to the hotel. Brittany slid in gracefully, placing her feet ever so gently inside.

"Happy Birthday!" Mina shouted.

"Thanks, girl."

"Mami, you look hot!"

Brittany blushed. "Thank you. So do you."

Mina rarely wore her hair down. Her long thick curls cascaded down her back. Her bright red lipstick perfectly matched her halter style dress. Brittany inspected the limo. It looked better without her parents in it. Black cushiony leather seats and soft white accents lights adorned the interior. "Chica, time to get our drink on!" Mina said, reaching for the liquor on the mini bar.

Brittany curled her left eyebrow into a frown. "Girl, please."

"We can take a little sip. Nobody will know."

"You don't know my parents."

"Well, I'm going to have some fun, Hollywood style!" Mina poured a half of a glass of Hennessey cognac.

"Girl, what are you doing? That's way too much!"

Mina looked around the limo. "I'm going to have to drink it because there's nowhere to pour it."

Brittany contorted her face into a nasty frown. She wished Mina would have just left the freakin' bottle alone.

"Fine, I'll pour it in the ice bucket."

"Whatever."

Mina poured the alcohol into the bucket, spilling some onto the black carpet.

"What are you doing?" Brittany snapped. "Just leave it!"

"You can't see it."

"You can smell it. If my parents get in here, I'm dead."

Mina took a large gulp, as if she were drinking water on a hot day, and started coughing uncontrollably. She regained her composure and tried to sit as elegantly as possible while the alcohol burned a hole in her throat and chest.

Brittany took her mind off Mina. That was her body, if she wanted to poison it, that was on her. She had more important matters to think about. It was after all, her sweet sixteenth birthday party. The one she had been dreaming of since she was a little girl.

When the limousine turned off Peachtree Street and into the hotel driveway, Brittany's nerves fell into her stomach. She couldn't believe her eyes. A cherry red carpet stretched from curbside to the entrance. People were standing outside the building, waiting. "Oh-my-God, the paparazzi is here!" Brittany squealed.

"Dang girl, this is tight!" Mina said. "You ready?"

Brittany drew in a deep breath. "Well, it's now or never. You go first."

With one hand tucked behind his back, the chauffeur opened the door with poise. Mina went first and then moved to the side to wait for the birthday girl. Brittany checked herself in her hand mirror, practiced her smile for the cameras, and stepped out gracefully. People were calling her name, but she was too afraid to look into the crowd. Cameras clicked and lights flashed wildly while she kept her focus on the hotel entrance. She walked slowly and elegantly, the way she and her mom had been practicing for weeks. "Happy Birthday, Brittany!" someone shouted.

She offered a beauty queen style wave to the crowd and then turned her attention back to the double doors she would soon enter. She wondered how her parents managed to get the paparazzi there and if her picture would really end up in the newspapers and on television, like Halle Berry at the premiere of one of her movies. As she made her way to the ballroom, Brittany looked up and caught her own image hanging high above the entrance doors—a huge poster that her parents had made from one of her glam photos taken over the summer. She was posed in an off the shoulder pink feather top. Brittany loved that picture. She couldn't ask for better parents. Yes, they were overbearing at times to the point where it seemed as though she had to ask for permission to breath, but they spared no expense for this special birthday party.

When Brittany entered the Piedmont ballroom, it was more beautiful than she envisioned. Three large chandeliers were suspended down the center aisle, their Austrian crystal dazzled, casting a warm glow over all her guests. Wall sconces offered an over-the-shoulder illumination of the well-dressed crowd. The music was booming. Kids were already on the dance floor waving hello and motioning her to come dance. Brittany greeted her parents and brother with hugs. Shaniqua, Natasha and Stephen came over. Brittany scanned the room for Marcus, but didn't see him. Everyone took turns hugging Brittany and wishing her happy birthday.

"Okay ladies, let's get a group picture with Brittany and her best friends," Mrs. Brown said.

Mina hugged up next to Brittany. Shaniqua and Natasha passed knowing looks to one another. They were thinking the same thing; Mina was not a part of the posse. She was a new friend and had no right to be in the picture. Natasha stood on the other side of Brittany and Shaniqua stood next to Natasha. There was no way Shaniqua was going to stand next to Mina. She had already decided there was something about her she just didn't like, but she couldn't put her finger on it. Mrs. Brown snapped a half roll of film, then passed the camera to her husband to continue while she chatted with one of the caterers.

Natasha struck a daring pose that she had learned in modeling class. "I'll have you all know I get paid for having my picture taken!"

Brittany and Shaniqua looked at each, stuck their index finger high in the air in front of Natasha and singsonged, "riiiiighhhht!"

Everybody cracked up laughing, including Natasha.

Several minutes later, when the girls finished their photo session, Natasha looked for Stephen, but she couldn't find him anywhere in the room. He was probably in the bathroom or getting them refreshments, she decided.

The DJ blended in TI's new song. "Oh, this is my jam," Brittany said. "Let's dance y'all!"

Shaniqua turned up the corner of her mouth. "Y'all go right ahead. Y'all know I don't dance with a bunch of girls."

Brittany, Natasha and Mina made their way to the dance floor. They were having a good time, when Brittany twirled around secretly looking for Marcus, but spotted Stephen instead. "Natasha, why's your man dancing with another girl?"

Natasha spun around, fierce like a tornado. "Brit,

that's the girl I've been telling you who's been starting crap with me."

Brittany shifted her weight to one foot and folded her hands across her chest. "What are you going to do?"

"I don't know. What should I do? It's not like I own him or something. We're not married—he can dance with whoever he wants to."

Mina rolled her eyes heavenward. "Better you than me, chica. He's stupid!"

"But why would Stephen do that when he knows how much that girl despises you?" Brittany asked.

Natasha shrugged. "I don't even know why she doesn't like me. I've never done anything to her, I don't even know her."

Mina took a step closer to Natasha. "Who gives a crap? The fact of the matter is she's dancing with your man! And it looks like he's enjoying himself. Look at the way she's dancing all up on him. If it were me, I wouldn't take that, chica."

Natasha threatened to tell her to shut the hell up, nobody asked for her opinion when Brittany's brother, Kevin, interrupted to dance with his sister. Natasha looked around for Shaniqua who was standing at the chocolate fountain dipping cookies into the sweet syrup. Anger swelled inside her as she made her way over.

"Tasha, what's wrong with you?" Shaniqua said, through a mouthful of cookies.

"Stephen's dancing with Kendra. Can you believe that crap?"

Shaniqua searched the crowd. "Where?"

Natasha pointed to the dance floor. Stephen was

smiling, looking as though he was thoroughly enjoying himself watching his partner gyrate her hips to the music.

"Hell-to-the-no! Why's he dancing with that skank? If I were you, I'd check that real proper-like!"

"I'm not going to go over there to embarrass myself," Natasha said, folding her arms across her chest.

"The song just changed and look, he ain't made no effort to get off the dance floor. If it were me, I'd go over there."

"Please, I'm not chasing up behind him. He knows that we came together, so if that's the way he wants to be, two can play that game."

Two songs later, Natasha watched Stephen and Kendra exit the dance floor. Kendra's friend, Jasmine, was waiting at the edge of the dance floor. They laughed and slapped high-fives. Stephen walked in the opposite direction, inspecting the crowd. Natasha hid behind the large, white Roman-style column. Talking to him was the last thing she wanted to do. If it wasn't for this being a special night for her best friend, she would call her dad or brother to come pick her up. Now she understood why her dad gave her that mad money, because right now, she was mad as hell, and nothing or no one was going to coerce her into riding home with Stephen.

Suddenly the music stopped, the dim lights turned bright, then went back low. An array of soft royal blue lights beamed onto the platform where Brittany's dad was standing. Dozens of tiny white decorative lights outlined the stage. An impressive, black grand piano sat center stage on the platform where an arc of silver and white balloons was suspended in the air. Mr. Brown tested the microphone. The buzz of conversation died down.

Natasha's eyes were fixed on the stage when she felt hands wrap around her waistline. She turned around slowly, stalling; she knew it was Stephen. She just wasn't sure how to respond. She felt like socking him in the jaw. Having grown up with two brothers, Natasha knew how and where to land a good punch. "What's up?" she said dryly, while gently removing his hands.

Stephen leaned in for a kiss on the lips, but caught Natasha's cheek instead. "Hey babe, I've been looking for you."

"Ladies and gentlemen," Mr. Brown said, "the birthday girl has prepared a special treat for you this evening. Join me in welcoming my daughter, the joy of my life, Brittany, to the stage."

A thunder of cheers and claps sounded.

"Stephen, please. Spare me. So I guess you decided on Kendra when you couldn't find me. Is that it?" Natasha took a few steps forward, moving away from him.

Brittany stepped on stage looking beautiful in a black Donna Karan fitted dressed. It was very different from the dull-black recital dresses that she used to wear when performing. Loose sexy curls hung about her shoulders, while chandelier earrings dangled from her ears. She sat down elegantly at the piano, her back erect, feet planted on the floor. The soft, regal glow from the blue lights made Brittany look like a well-seasoned performer. Using a Hanon exercise that she learned years ago, Brittany warmed her fingers and calmed her nerves. Its staccato rhythm sounded like a song. The crowd applauded.

Stephen tugged at Natasha's arm. "Wait, Tasha. I can explain."

She cut her eyes at him, silencing him.

Brittany played the first few bars of Alicia's Keys' "Fallin." The crowd went wild.

Natasha and Shaniqua moved away from Stephen and made their way to the front of the stage. Brittany's fingers danced gracefully on the keys. She had been studying classical piano since the age of three. It was a relief for her to play something contemporary and fun, to play for her crowd. She poured her heart into the song. The crowd was mesmerized.

Antonio, "The Queen," as he called himself, stood next to Natasha and Shaniqua with closed eyes, swaying narrow hips, bellowing instead of singing. His voice was piercing and off key. Shaniqua frowned. "Dang, he needs to shut the heck up!" Antonio continued singing, growing louder and gyrating his hips harder. His arms were flailing through the air. Shaniqua leaned over to him and tapped him on the shoulder. "Uh, excuse me."

He spun around with a fierce, annoyed expression on his face. His electric blue contacts stood out like two small glow-in-the-dark balls. "Yes," he said, his voice was unusually high.

"Who sings this song?" Shaniqua asked.

Antonio rolled his eyes and pursed his lips with attitude. "Alicia Keys."

"You need to let her sing it!"

Shaniqua and Natasha cracked up laughing and moved away from him so they could enjoy Brittany's performance. The crowd applauded and cheered when the song ended. Brittany's dad greeted her on the stage and escorted her down to the floor and over to her handsomely decorated cake.

Brittany discreetly scanned the area for Marcus and when she finally spotted him, he blew her a kiss that made her blush. She played it off by focusing on her cake. She didn't want to give her parents anything to talk about, worry about, and most of all, another reason to treat her like a prisoner. Marcus was standing next to Carlos and Mina. Brittany wanted badly to invite him over, but she knew that was asking for trouble. Her mom was on one side, her dad on the other as the crowd began to sing "Happy Birthday." Brittany couldn't believe that they were actually singing to her. That was so nine-year-oldish. Her parents were definitely corny. Brittany had to regain some coolness, so she stood looking brazen, with one hand on her round hip while the other one toyed with her hair, flipping a meddling curl around. There was no way she was about to sing she was sixteen. That was simply ridiculous.

Brittany grabbed the silver plated cake cutter. It was almost too beautiful to eat—shaped like a stack of birthday presents, each boxlike cake was a different flavor. Brittany's favorite was carrot cake and was the largest of the presents, decorated in sea green with a pink bow on it.

When everyone had their fill of cake, Mr. Brown motioned for the crowd to follow him outside. Brittany was beaming from ear to ear. She had been waiting for this moment for years. She could hardly contain her excitement. The car of her dreams was only a few yards away. Brittany turned around to see Marcus trailing behind her, along with Natasha, Shaniqua, Mina, Carlos and the rest of the crowd. Her heart pounded as she pushed open the heavy door, making her way outside. Knowing her parents, they had chosen white, silver or green. Her dad insisted that a black car was too grown-up looking. Her eyes fell on a shiny, new emerald green Honda Accord with a large pink ribbon strapped to the roof. Some kids clapped, others whistled, while some sniggered. Time stood still. Brittany could no longer hear the screams and whistles. Her ears had stopped working. Her face was frozen, expressionless. She watched her dad pull open the driver's car door. Tears blurred her vision. She clasped her hands over her eyes. She felt her mother's slender arms around her shoulders. Brittany's mouth fell open in shock, but her words of protest died in her throat.

"Oh, Brittany, we're so glad that you like it. Sit down, dear. Try it out. Mommy knew you'd love that AKA Ivy green."

The crowd chanted, "Brittany! Brittany! Brittany!"

She wished they'd shut the hell up. This was the absolute lowest point in her life. How could her parents do that to her? Everyone knew that she was supposed to get a Lexus. Now she looked like a fool, a lame duck. She hated her parents. They stood next to the car, grinning—proud as two dirty peacocks.

Chapter 20

After the party, Natasha and Shaniqua waited outside the hotel for Natasha's brother to pick them up. Natasha rested against the brick building looking for her dad's old Buick to come rolling up. Her feet were aching along with her heart. She hoped Nate wouldn't start asking a bunch of unnecessary questions. "Alright, Shaniqua, when we get in the car, do not mention anything about Stephen, okay?"

"Fine. But if I were you, I would tell him what happened."

"Why? This has nothing to do with him."

"Well, I wish I had an older brother to take up for me."

"I can handle this myself. I don't need Nate dippin' in my business, then running back telling my dad and God only knows who else."

"Fine, whatever," Shaniqua said and turned her attention to the street. "Hey, Granny told me that the name Peachtree came from "pitch tree."

Natasha sneered. "Number one, who cares, and two,

uh Georgia is the 'Peach state'."

"Granny told me that there's no historical tree that led to the name Peachtree. It was a pitch tree; somehow the translation or whatever got messed up."

Natasha cocked her head in disbelief.

"I swear you and Brittany think y'all know everything."

Natasha looked up and saw Nate pulling into the circular driveway. "Here he is now."

Shaniqua hopped into the back seat. "Hey Nate," she said, soft and flirtatiously. Natasha shot Shaniqua a don't-play-look. Shaniqua grinned mischievously.

"What's up?" Nate said, his voice was deep and serious. He looked over to Natasha in the front seat next to him. "What happened to Stephen?"

"Nothing. He had to leave early," Natasha offered. "Mom sleep?"

"She was when I left."

Good. That way she wouldn't have to explain anything to her mother. Natasha thought of taking the portrait down as soon as she walked through the front door, but decided against it. That—she would have to explain. Her mom loved that portrait from the moment she first laid eyes on it last Christmas.

Brittany trailed her parents' home in her new car, angry

about her Lexus, angry that she couldn't hang out with Marcus. She had only spent a few minutes with him at the party. It was a shame she had to hide him from her parents. But she knew how they would have responded. "He's too old for you, Brittany. And you're too young to date anyway." Marcus was a good guy by any parents' standards, except hers. He was a senior football player and he made good grades in school. And he didn't drink or smoke and planned on being a sports therapist after college.

Suddenly, Brittany reached in her purse for her cell phone to officially break rule number one: talking on the cell while driving. She dialed Marcus's number.

"What's up?" he said.

Brittany giggled. "Nothing."

"Where are you? I thought we were going to kick it a little after your party."

"I know, but my mom wasn't feeling well, and my dad stayed afterwards to handle some business."

"Man, your moms is like always sick."

"I know, I'm sorry."

"It's like we're supposed to be kickin it, but we never spend any time together. This isn't working for me. You don't have time for me."

Brittany fell silent. No words would come to mind. He was right. They hardly ever spent time together. Their relationship existed mostly over the telephone. They attended different schools. Marcus always had football practice while Brittany was at cheerleading practice. On Friday nights after their games, they hooked up for a few minutes before Brittany had to be home and that was only if her parents didn't come to the games with her. "I know, Marcus, you're right. I'm going to work on changing it."

"When you work it out, let me know," he said and hung up before Brittany could say anything.

She snapped her hot pink Razr phone shut and threw it against the passenger seat. It bounced off the black leather seat and fell to the floor. Tears trickled down her face. This was never supposed to happen on her sixteenth birthday. Her parents were ruining her life and they needed to know it. Brittany turned into the driveway, haphazardly parked the car on the grass, yanked the keys out of the ignition and stormed into the house. "Mom!"

Yelling in the house was forbidden and carried a sentence of at least a day's punishment.

Mrs. Brown came running from the kitchen. "Brittany, what on earth is the matter? Why are you crying? Did you have an accident? Are you okay?"

"I'm fine. Where's Daddy?"

"He's upstairs getting ready for bed. What's the problem, are you hurt?"

"No. I mean, yes."

"What's going on down there?" Brittany's dad called out and stood at the top of the stairs, with a pipe clamped in the corner of his mouth.

Mrs. Brown looked up. "I don't know what's wrong with her."

"I'm sick of you guys treating me like a baby! I can't ever hang out with my friends. You guys take me to the games like I'm twelve," Brittany said, watching her dad take slow methodical steps down the stairs.

Her heart fluttered. She had never spoken to her parents this way, but she had come too far to turn back now. If she was going to be grounded for life, she might as well let them know how she felt.

Mr. Brown began puffing on his pipe, no doubt arranging his opinions in his mind. When he reached the bottom stair, he removed the pipe from his lips. "Repeat the part about us treating you like a child."

Brittany could feel the vibration of her heart pounding like the bass of a drum, da-dum da-dum.

He studied his pipe and then turned back to Brittany. "Please correct me if I'm wrong, but I didn't know that twelve-year-olds received brand new cars? Do they?"

"I didn't get the car that I wanted."

Mr. Brown offered Brittany a look as if she were a Martian visiting from outer space. He turned his attention to Brittany's mom. "Sheila, I had no idea our child was this ungrateful." He turned back to Brittany. "When I was your age, I would have been glad if someone had given me a bicycle, better yet, food. If it hadn't been for your mom, you never would have had this party. I didn't do it for your brother and you didn't deserve it. Not with the behavior you've been demonstrating."

"Humph!" Brittany said.

Mr. Brown glared at his daughter, closing in on her. "I'm only going to say this once, so hear me clearly. Change your attitude. That car can still go back." He stared at her for a few seconds longer, letting his anger permeate the air, and then looked to his wife. "Now, young lady, I think you owe your mom and me an apology."

"Sorry," Brittany said, doing her best to mask the sarcasm in her voice and then stormed up to her bedroom. Trying to tell her parents anything never worked. She would just have to show her parents with her actions. She wasn't going to let them ruin her relationship with Marcus.

Chapter 21

Monday afternoon, Shaniqua sat her lunch tray down. "What's so funny?"

"Nothing, we're just talking about my party. Tasha said I showed out on the piano."

Shaniqua nodded, "Yeah, girl you did your thang!"

Brittany struck a pose. "Thank you. Who's the goddess?"

"See, Brit, that's why nobody can ever pay you a compliment. You too conceited!" Shaniqua said, still smiling.

"I'm not conceited, just convinced, get on my level!"

Shaniqua's smile faded. "Whatever!"

"I see Mina and Carlos were together. Did you ever ask her if he hits her?" Natasha asked.

Brittany leaned in and whispered, "Y'all have not heard this from me, because I'm not one to gossip, but yes."

Natasha shook her head. "That's so sad."

Shaniqua turned up her nose. "Sad, that's stupid to let some boy beat on you."

"No, what I'm saying is, she thinks that she has to take it from him and she doesn't." Natasha turned to Brittany. "You really need to talk to her."

"I tried a few weeks ago and you see she's still with him, so that's her business."

Shaniqua faced Brittany. "If you're such good friends like you claim, what's the problem? You don't hesitate to get all up in my mix."

"What mix? You don't have anything going on." Brittany said.

Shaniqua frowned. "You don't know everything about me."

"I know enough," Brittany responded.

"Y'all please stop," Natasha said, turning her attention to Brittany. "How do you like your new ride, girl?"

Shaniqua cackled. "Yeah, Brittany, how's your new Lexus?"

"At least I have a car," Brittany retorted, "What do you have, run over stilettos? Ooops, I'm sorry you don't even have those, they're your cousin's."

Natasha looked up from her burger. "Brittany, here comes your girl?"

"Oh, great, our newfound fourth member," Shaniqua added.

"Hey, chicas," Mina said, sitting down with books in her hand.

Brittany and Natasha both responded, while Shaniqua pretended to be busy eating lunch. Shaniqua never ate; she only grabbed a tray every day because she received free lunch.

"Brittany, your party was hot! You and Marcus look so cute dancing together. How are things going with you guys? You never hang out with me and Carlos anymore."

Shaniqua grunted.

Brittany shot Shaniqua a look to silence her and then turned to Mina. "My man is fine, thank you very much," Brittany said. There was no way she was about to tell her girls that he dumped her the night of her birthday party.

Shaniqua rolled her eyes. "Puh-leeze, he's not all that."

"Jealousy will get you nowhere, my friend," Brittany said, laughing.

Shaniqua smirked. "Jealous of who, what?"

"We all have boyfriends and you have—none!" Brittany sneered.

Suddenly a group of girls walked over to the table. "Uh, which one of y'all is Natasha?" one of them said.

When Natasha turned around, she saw Kendra and a few other girls whose names she didn't know. Her heart raced. "I am."

"Why are you going around telling everyone that I tried to take your man at the party?"

Natasha puckered her brow creating a deep furrow. "Excuse me?"

Kendra took a step closer to Natasha. "You heard me, I didn't stutter."

Natasha couldn't believe this was happening. She wondered why this Beyonce look-a-like reject was standing in her face starting mess. "I didn't tell anybody that."

"For your information, if I wanted yo' man, I would

take him."

Natasha hesitated while the palms of her hands grew moist. She couldn't believe she was actually getting ready to fight, and especially over a guy. She stared at Kendra, trying to decide how to handle the situation. The entire lunchroom was watching. If she did nothing, then everyone would think they could run over her. But if she hit the girl, then everyone would say that she was fighting over a guy, not to mention she would get in trouble. Natasha stood up, towering over Kendra by at least five inches. Students who were aware that something out of the ordinary was about to happen poked one another to shut up and watch. The cafeteria suddenly grew quiet. Natasha took a step forward when she heard the school resource officers pushing through the crowd. "Break it up, break it up! There's nothing to see here," one of them said as he got in between Kendra and Natasha.

The round ended when the bell rang.

Brittany turned to Natasha with a worried look on her face. "Girl, are you alright? Would you like for me and Mina to walk you to class?"

"No, of course not, I'm fine. Kendra's the one that better be worried."

"If it were me, she would have gotten the beat down," Shaniqua said.

Brittany pursed her lips. "Please, you had your chance with Cherise."

"The only reason I didn't was because I was pregnant."

Everyone said their goodbyes and scattered.

Natasha made her way to class, fury brewing inside her. She heard the hushed whispers and buzz around her as she walked purposefully through the corridor. She saw the curious stares, but ignored them. Her mind was on Stephen. She dreaded seeing him, so much so that she didn't want to come to school. She hadn't spoken to him since Saturday night at the party. She had refused his ride home that night and refused his phone calls all day Sunday.

When Natasha made it to art class, a note was on her seat. She discreetly opened it and slid it under her art folder so Mr. Arnold would not see it.

Dear Natasha,

I know this is very uncharacteristic of me, writing you a letter, but I just want to express how deeply sorry I am for my actions Saturday night. I can only imagine how you must feel about me right now. I would like a chance to explain things. I know what you think you saw, but that's not exactly how things happened. I guess what I'm trying to say is please don't give up on me. If you give me another chance, I promise it will never happen again. Can we please talk after school? If you say no, then I apologize and will never bother you again. I'll understand. It's just my loss.

Always,

Stephen

Stephen's words were weighing heavy on Natasha like bricks. Her heart told her to give him another chance, but her head said no. Especially after she watched Shaniqua get played last year, and people were still talking about it. Kendra was causing too much drama between them. She wondered if he was secretly giving Kendra ammunition. There was no way she was going to let any brother think that he could disrespect her and get away with it, not even for a minute. The more Natasha thought about it, the angrier she grew. She wanted to leave the classroom; sitting so close to him enraged her. Mr. Arnold was busy discussing the color wheel and unraveling the mysteries of color as students worked on their drawings. Suddenly, Mr. Arnold appeared at her workstation. "Natasha, why aren't you drawing?"

She hesitated to answer. It wasn't like she could say, "Because I'm mad at my ex-boyfriend." She didn't have an excuse. Her eyes traveled down to her hands resting in her lap, "I'm sorry, Mr. Arnold, I hurt my hand yesterday."

Mr. Arnold studied Natasha, searching for truth in her eyes. "Where's your note from your parent?"

She shrugged her shoulders at first, but then she realized that would not work. She had to come up with something quick. "I thought it would be okay, but I've been using it all day—writing in my other classes and now it's aching again."

"Alright, the next time I'll need a note from your parents, otherwise I will have no choice but to give you a zero for class participation," Mr. Arnold said, then he went searching for another victim.

Natasha sat there studying the clock. Out of the corner of her eye, she could see Stephen trying to make eye contact. She wasn't going to give him the satisfaction of looking her in the eyes. She stared at the clock. It was almost three-thirty. She kept her eyes glued to the red second hand, waiting for the dismissal bell. She intended to race out the door with lightning speed to get away from Stephen.

When the bell chimed, Natasha sprang from her seat, grabbed her backpack and bolted for the door. Her foot looped through her purse strap that was lying on the floor, sending her flying head first to the floor. Her body followed, collapsing in front of the doorway. She was devastated. The word embarrassed could never describe how she felt. Death was the only thing that could ease the pain. She heard a barrage of voices in nightmarish slow motion, 'Arrree yooouuu oookkaaay?" but she couldn't focus on any one person. Her thoughts were rampant. There was no way she could really be sprawled out in the floor in the doorway. It had to be a dream. No, a nightmare. Reality sat in. *Ho, ho, ho, Green Giant.* No, she was worse than the Jolly Green Giant, she thought, at least he never fell.

Stephen came into focus. She saw the little locks in his hair as he bent down to gather her belongings. She felt his hand on her arm, removing her from the doorway. She would have smacked him if she had an ounce of dignity left. He had no right to touch her. "Are you okay?" he said.

Natasha nodded, the fall had temporarily silenced her. She slid a strand of hair behind her ear in an attempt to restore an air of dignity. "I'm fine," she said, brushing her glittered-speckled jeans. She picked up her purse and made her way through the door. *Ho ho ho, Green Giant!*

Stephen trailed her out the classroom. "Tasha, are you okay?"

"Yes! Now, leave me be."

"Just give me two minutes to explain. Please."

To compensate for the embarrassment that she suffered, she reacted with extreme attitude. She tucked her arms tightly across her chest and looked down at her watch. "Speak!"

"I'm very sorry about Saturday night, but it wasn't my fault. I was just trying to help someone out."

Natasha rolled her eyes. "Someone like who, Kendra?"

"Yes, she said her ex-boyfriend was there and she wanted him to see her dancing with someone so that he would leave her alone. I guess he's been stalking her or something."

"Stephen, that's so lame. You can't be that freakin' naïve. She's playing you like a freakin' fiddle. She hates me and she wants to get with you, don't you see that?"

A slight smile crept across Stephen's face. "Really?"

"I don't find that very amusing! She's starting a lot of mess and she's about to get her feelings hurt and her head cracked!"

Stephen was still smiling.

"What's so damn funny?"

"You look cute when you're angry. I've never seen you angry before."

"And you never will again!" Natasha took off down

the hallway.

"Wait! Tasha," he said, taking off after her. "You're absolutely right. Next time, I'll just tell her that she needs to find someone else."

"No, not the next time, you go find her and tell her that you have a girlfriend and that you don't have time for her silly little games."

Stephen smiled. "So, you still my girl?"

Natasha stared at his plump pink lips. She didn't want to smile at him, but she couldn't hold back any longer. His hazel eyes were the most sincere she had seen. "Just don't pull that crap again!"

"I won't, I promise," Stephen said, moving closer. "Now give me a kiss."

"I'm not kissing you here in front of everybody."

"Okay, at least give me a hug."

Natasha quickly scanned the vicinity to see if her brother was around. The last thing she needed was for Nate to report to their dad that she was hugged up in the hallways. She wrapped her slender arms around his waist, while Stephen planted a soft kiss on her cheek. Secretly, she hoped that Kendra or her cronies saw them. Natasha glanced at her watch. "I'll walk over to your locker with you."

"What for?" Stephen said.

"Because I want you to tell Kendra what's up."

"Don't you have to meet your brother at the car?"

Natasha shifted her weight to her other leg. "Nate can wait. It's not like he can leave without me. I want this mess squashed today."

Stephen jammed his hands in his front pockets.

"Tasha, it's really not that serious."

Natasha felt a new rush of fury course through her, her eyes darted back and forth between Stephen's eyes. "It's not that serious." Natasha slapped her hands against her narrow hips and let them rest there. "Not that serious for who? I'll tell you what, when you decide to step up and let her know what time it is, that's when you call me. Otherwise, don't bother!" she said and stormed away.

Chapter 22

Brittany spotted Marcus's truck in the school parking lot at Stephen High. She pulled up behind it to wait for him. Marcus walked to his truck wearing a black skullcap snug over his head. Brittany honked the horn and waved him over. She rolled down the car window. "Hey there," she said, her dimples dancing.

"What's up? What are you doing here?" he said, a serious edge to his voice.

"I would like to talk to you. Can you get in for a minute?"

Marcus left his gym bag outside the car and slid into the passenger seat. "What's up?"

Brittany let out a nervous giggle. "I just wanted to say that I'm sorry for not spending a lot of time with you. Now that I have my own car, it'll be different. What do you say?"

Marcus locked eyes with Brittany. "For real?"

"Yes, I'm here, aren't I?" Brittany giggled.

He smiled and leaned in for a kiss.

All week, it had worked out perfectly. Brittany's

parents allowed her to come home an hour later each evening because she told them that Coach Felder said that they would need the extra practice time to get ready for a cheerleading competition. Brittany and Marcus spent their evenings in the car, sitting cheek to cheek, feeling one another's love through the fabric of their clothes. Kisses made long and sweet. It became love's ritual.

Throughout the game Friday night, Brittany's mind was on Marcus. She couldn't care less that the Miller Grove Vikings were playing the number one school, East Lithonia, and it showed in her cheering. She had trouble keeping time with the chants. Her mind was on the after game festivities, in which she and Marcus had plans to meet—their first official date.

Brittany sipped a forbidden soda at the burger joint, waiting for Marcus to show. What her parents didn't know, wouldn't hurt. She was going to do what she wanted. It was her parents' choice if they chose not to drink carbonated beverages because of its supposed inability to be processed through the body. She happened to like it—like it very much. Glancing around the restaurant's simple red and white décor, she tapped her nails on the table, waiting. The clock read 9:42 p.m. She wondered if she should call Marcus, but she didn't want to appear uptight. She would give him until ten o'clock, then she'd have to leave in order to make it home by curfew.

At 9:55, Marcus came strolling through the doors. His jeans hung well, not too tight, and not sloppily down under his butt like a thug. His orange polo shirt contrasted nicely against his medium brown complexion. Even his low-top white sneakers looked cute. Everything was cute about Marcus. Brittany made a mental note to snap his picture with her camera phone so she could look at him whenever she wanted. Marcus made his way over to the table. "What's up?"

"Hey, what's up? What took so long?"

"I had to shower. What's the rush?"

Brittany let her eyes fall to her watch. "Well, I don't have all night."

"Alright, here we go again," Marcus said, shaking his head. "I knew this was a bad idea. Every time we get together, we're always rushing."

Brittany giggled. "I'm not rushing. I just asked what took so long, because I missed seeing you, that's all," she said sweetly. To mask the irritation she felt, she batted her eyelashes.

"Cool. So what do you want to get into tonight?"

Brittany shrugged. She hated to tell him that she had to be home in thirty minutes. Why did her parents put her under all this stress? The least they could do was let her stay out until eleven. For goodness sakes, she was sixteen with her own ride.

"We'll eat, then go for a ride or something. Maybe

cruise Peachtree Street strip," he offered, picking up a menu.

"I'm not hungry."

"Well, I'm starving."

Marcus ordered his food and by 10:20 he was eating it. Brittany was stuck. Her parents or Marcus? Marcus or her parents? Marcus. She discreetly turned her cell phone on vibrate and watched Marcus chow down on his burger. She wished she had ordered one too, but girls didn't look cute chowing down giant size burgers. Snacking on fries was the more appropriate choice. She ordered Cajun fries and relaxed into conversation about Marcus's football game.

When they finished eating, it was 10:45 p.m. The server brought the bill and set it face down on the table. Brittany waited for Marcus to grab the check. Several minutes passed before he picked it up. "Hey "B," can you get this? I'm tapped out."

"Sure." She dug around in her Dooney & Bourke bag for her wallet. Now she knew with extreme clarity that her parents would not approve of Marcus. Her dad always said that it was the male's responsibility to court the female, not the other way around.

"So, you want to take a drive down by Piedmont Park?"

"I guess so," she said, smiling sweetly, though she really didn't want to drive almost twenty miles away.

"Cool, can I drive your whip? My truck burns too much gas."

"I don't know about that. My dad doesn't want anyone else driving my car."

"Is it your car or your dad's?"

"It's mine."

"Then let me drive your whip."

Brittany's mind raced back to her dad. He always said that she would not be allowed to drive boys around, but he never said they couldn't drive her in her car. Brittany giggled. "Alright, don't do anything stupid."

Marcus offered her a big dopey-eyed puppy dog smile. "What? You don't trust me?"

Brittany tried to conceal her smile, but it was useless. If she was going to get in trouble tonight, she might as well have fun.

Marcus held Brittany's hand in his and drove with the other one. Brittany opened the sunroof, her hair blowing in the wind. The night air felt good, like freedom hovering around her and all she had to do was grab it. She felt so grown-up cruising down I-20 West. Marcus parked the car across the street from the park. The streetlights cast an angelic glow, setting a romantic mood. They chatted briefly about music, then Marcus motioned for Brittany to move closer. They wasted little time getting reacquainted. They kissed until their jaws ached. Marcus pulled away gently. "So what's up?"

Brittany looked confused. "What are you talking about?"

Marcus grinned. "You know. Let's take it to the next level."

"Are you crazy? I'm not getting busy with you. I'm not giving up my goodies like that."

"I didn't say you had to, but you can still take care of me."

Brittany scrunched her face. “Take care of you?”

Marcus looked down in his lap and smiled. “That way we’ll both be satisfied and you get to keep your virginity.”

❧

When Marcus turned the car back on the neon clock’s green numbers said 11:47, Brittany’s heart nearly collapsed.

“What’s the matter?” Marcus said.

“Uh, well, I was supposed to be home.”

“Tell your parents the game let out late and everybody went to the same place to eat so it took your food a long time.”

“You don’t know my parents. That’ll never work.”

“What time were you supposed to be home?”

Brittany looked out the window for the answer; she caught her reflection in the mirror. Things were going so well with Marcus. She wondered if she could trust him enough to tell him the truth. She really liked him. He was cute, funny and smart. His only drawback was not picking up the check tonight.

“What time were you supposed to be home?” Marcus repeated.

“Ten-thirty.”

“Ten-thirty? The games are barely over by then. That’s whack!”

"I know. But those are my parents' rules, so we need to go now. I'll drive myself," Brittany said, quickly opening the car door.

Marcus sat in the passenger seat, shaking his head. "This ain't cool. I was looking for someone to hang out and kick it a little—someone to be my girlfriend."

Brittany gripped the steering wheel tightly and stared straight ahead. She knew exactly where Marcus was going with this. He was going to say the same stuff he had said over the telephone. She braced herself by concentrating on the road. She was not going to give him the satisfaction of seeing her cry. He was not worth it, she told herself. The silence between them was stifling.

When Brittany pulled up behind Marcus's truck, he opened the passenger door. Brittany could tell that he was waiting for her to look at him. "This ain't working, Brittany."

She glared at him. His words hurt, but she bit back the pain. "Fine. Not a problem."

Marcus got out of the car and closed the door. Brittany sped off, fighting back the tears. When she was safely out of eyesight, she let them flow. She didn't know why she was crying. It wasn't like she was in love with him. They hardly knew one another.

When Brittany arrived home, all the lights on the first level of the house were on. She sat in the car trying to concoct a good story, but she knew nothing would work. Her dad would read her like an open book. Her parents must have heard the car pull up because they came running out of the house. Mrs. Brown wrapped her arm around Brittany's shoulder. "Oh, baby, are you okay?"

Brittany nodded.

Mr. Brown inspected the exterior of the car and then studied his daughter. "Where the hell have you been?"

Brittany locked eyes with him. She had never seen him this angry, except when her brother Kevin failed the eighth grade. Kevin had handed his dad the report card nonchalantly. The words "Student Retained" stamped in bright red lettering jumped out at Mr. Brown. He threw the paper down, took his thick black leather belt off and in one smooth, swift motion and began to whip Kevin right there in the formal living room. Mr. Brown had worked hard all his life to achieve his success, starting with a paper route when he was twelve years old and worked two jobs to put his self through medical school. The last thing he wanted was for his children to disgrace his good name and undo all of his hard work. Brittany hoped he wasn't going to do the same thing to her now, though he had never spanked her before. Mr. Brown closed in on Brittany, towering over her. He was so close she could smell the sweet musk of his aftershave. "Don't make me ask you again, young lady."

"Nowhere," Brittany blurted out and then burst into tears.

Mrs. Brown motioned for Brittany to hurry into the house.

"Don't insult my intelligence, Brittany."

"I met a friend after the game and we just grabbed a bite to eat. That's all."

"What time is it?"

Brittany looked at her wristwatch through teary eyes. "Almost twelve-thirty."

"And what time where you supposed to be home?"

"Ten-thirty," Brittany muttered.

"Don't mumble. I see you're not ready for the responsibility that we've given you."

"I am too ready. You guys don't trust me."

"Are you worthy of trust?"

"Yes. I've never done anything and you treat me like a prisoner."

Mr. Brown placed his index finger over his mouth. "Hmmm, let's see what has Brittany done?" He removed his finger. "For an honor student with good grades, you certainly aren't acting like you have the good sense that God gave you. Give me your car keys and cell phone, and go to bed!"

Brittany stared at her dad in shock. The hurt she felt was devastating. She might as well have been beaten.

Chapter 23

Monday morning, Brittany slumped quietly in the seat of her father's car all the way to school. She didn't want anyone to see him dropping her off. She needed to think of a lie that she could tell when people asked why she wasn't driving herself in her own car. When Mr. Brown pulled up in front of the school, Brittany opened the car door before he made a complete stop, and dashed out. She scurried into the building before anyone could say anything. She was angry at her parents and Marcus. Brittany ducked into the bathroom, restyled her hair and applied makeup—her usual morning ritual—and then met her friends. "Hey y'all," Brittany said dryly.

"What's wrong with you?" Shaniqua asked.

"Y'all don't tell anybody, but my dad took away my car and my cell phone."

Natasha furrowed her brow. "Why?"

"I hung out too late Friday night with Marcus."

"How late?" Natasha asked.

"After midnight."

Shaniqua nudged Brittany. "Hey, hot Momma, what

did y'all do?"

Brittany smiled bashfully.

Shaniqua gasped. "Did y'all get busy?"

"No, we didn't have sex . . . but,"

Shaniqua squealed, "But what?"

Brittany offered a mysterious look, then giggled.

Natasha scrunched her face in disbelief. "Y'all did that?"

Brittany giggled.

Shaniqua cupped her hand over her mouth. "Brittany's having sex, oh-my-God, I don't believe it!"

Brittany frowned. "That's not sex!"

"Brittany, oral sex is sex!" Shaniqua said loudly.

"No, it's not!"

Natasha nodded. "Yes, it is Brit."

Shaniqua shivered. "Eeeuww! That's just nasty!"

Brittany snickered. "Well, at least I don't have to worry about getting pregnant."

"No, but you can still get an STD," Shaniqua said.

Natasha interjected, "Did Marcus use a condom?"

"No, but I'm not worried because he did not ejaculate in my mouth, for your information."

"Oh ho ho," Shaniqua chimed, "Ms. Smarty-pants don't know everything. Babygirl, there's such a thing as pre-cum fluids, and they can get into your mouth and infect you if you have an open sore or cut in your mouth. Trust me, they told me about all that stuff last year at the clinic."

Brittany huffed. "Well, I'm not worried about it. One, I don't have an open sore or cut in my mouth—"

"That you know of!" Shaniqua interjected.

"And two, Marcus and I are through!"

Natasha shot Shaniqua a curious look and then looked at Brittany. "Girl, what happened?"

Brittany shook her head. "He said that I didn't have enough time for him."

Shaniqua burst into a boisterous cackle. "Ahhh, you got dumped!"

"I did not!"

Natasha shot Shaniqua a look that ceased the laughter. "Girl, are you alright?" Natasha asked with genuine concern.

Brittany flipped her long mane behind her shoulder. "Girl, please, no love lost here! I'm going to focus on gaining my parents' trust so I can get my car back. How's Stephen?"

Natasha shrugged. "I'm not talking to him!" she said, glancing at the clock on the wall in the commons area. "Y'all want to eat a light lunch today and then go to a buffet or something after school? I drove today, Nate's at home sick."

"I can't," Brittany said, "I've got cheerleading practice."

"Me, either," Shaniqua said. "I'm trying to get a job, so I'm going to the mall to put in applications."

"Good luck, I'll catch y'all on the rebound if you can get up!" Natasha said mimicking a basketball lay-up.

Shaniqua smirked. "Funny, hardy-har-har!"

Chapter 24

That afternoon Shaniqua headed to Stonecrest Mall, determined to get a job. She had been thinking about it for weeks. Stonecrest, one of the largest malls in DeKalb County, had at least a hundred stores. Shaniqua walked the shopping mall until her feet throbbed, traveling from store to store—every department store, clothing store, knickknack shop and eatery, filling out countless applications. The only ones she skipped were men's stores. She didn't want to come into contact with boys unnecessarily. Rarely did a day pass that some boy didn't try to holla, "Let me tap that…" "Can a player get in them guts…" "I'll tear yo' back out or I got five on it!" She was beginning to hate boys more and more. Maybe all men were no good.

The next day, much to her surprise, Shaniqua received a phone call from the cookie store requesting an interview. She excitedly scheduled the appointment for the following day after school. Dressed in tight dark-rinsed jeans, a black fitted t-shirt and matching stilettos, Shaniqua hurried to the mall for her first job interview.

She was so anxious that she chewed gum to calm her nerves. When she arrived, the manager, Jack, ushered her into the back storeroom. The aroma of freshly baked goodies enticed her. Her eyes stole over to a warm tray of chocolate chip cookies. She could already taste the sweet melted morsels gliding down her throat. She wondered if Jack would give her a sample after the interview.

Jack's dark hair, friendly brown eyes and welcoming smile made him appear to be in his early twenties. Shaniqua relaxed in her seat and continued chewing gum; she could tell Jack had an easy way about him. He reviewed her application while she looked at the large commercial freezers and a mound of empty boxes stashed along the wall. Jack peered up from the application. "So, do you have any cash handling experience?"

Shaniqua nodded. "I use cash to buy everything, I don't even have a credit card."

The manager looked perplexed. "I'm sorry, as it relates to work experience."

Embarrassment washed over her. "No, sir."

"Do you prefer to work alone or as part of a team?

Shaniqua grinned. "Team."

"Because we're a small operation here, many times you'll be required to work alone," Jack said, scribbling on a notebook. "How do you feel about school?"

"I can't wait for it to end."

"What do you want to do after you graduate?"

She shrugged. "I don't know, maybe go to cosmetology school."

When the interview was over, Shaniqua left feeling uneasy. Jack had kept the questions short, like he was rushing. She wasn't sure how the interview went because she didn't have anything to compare it to.

The next day, Shaniqua was at home catching up on homework when the telephone rang. "Hello," she said.

"Hello, Shaniqua, please," A male's voice said.

Her heart thumped. "This is Shaniqua."

"This is Jack Callaway from Doughboy Cookies. I wanted to let you know that we've decided to go with someone else. You weren't exactly what we were looking for, but I'd like to encourage you to try us again after you have obtained some work experience."

As soon as she hung up the phone, she sat down on the sofa, her bottom sinking to the floor. Her shoulders curled in defeat. She glanced at the snapshot sitting on the coffee table of her and Granny one Christmas morning taken years ago. She had a good Christmas that year thanks to the church. Getting a job wasn't going to be as easy as everyone had suggested. She couldn't afford to give up. Suddenly, she wiggled her way out of the sunken couch. She had a great idea. The following day, she would spend her lunch hour visiting with Mrs. Smith, the guidance counselor to better prepare for the next job interview.

Shaniqua drew in a deep breath before she entered the

guidance counselor's office. All the students thought Mrs. Smith was loony because rarely did a student visit without her carrying on about her three degrees plastered on the walls. And if Mrs. Smith was feeling really good, she would talk about her husband, the doctor. She'd say, "And I have to watch out for them women in the church. They think I don't know they want my husband because he's a doctor. But I'm Ms. Clever, I see it all. You see, I've got three degrees."

Shaniqua knocked on the half-open door. A tiny hand beckoned her in. Mrs. Smith sat in the large desk chair like a miniature doll eating lunch. She was an elfin woman, just a few inches over four feet. Her face was small and birdlike while her hair resembled a large, curly afro from the 1970s. "Hi, Mrs. Smith, how are you?"

"God is good. I'm too blessed to be stressed." Mrs. Smith pecked at her pickle. "What can I do for you?"

Shaniqua saw the infamous three degrees hanging from the wall, an associate's, a bachelor's and a master's degree. A host of religious quotes and parables decorated the other walls. A black nativity set took center stage in the middle of her bookshelf. "Can you please help me with job interviews?"

Mrs. Smith looked up her from her plate and smiled. Her teeth resembled little yellow Chiclets. "I'm sure I can. Now, what type of job is it?"

"Well, I don't actually have an interview now. I just want to be prepared when someone else calls."

Mrs. Smith dipped celery into a small container of dressing. "I see, so you've already been on one?"

"Yes, ma'am."

"Interviews are like anything else in life, they take practice to perfect. You see, I have three degrees, therefore . . ."

Shaniqua studied her fingernails, waiting patiently until Mrs. Smith descended from her soapbox. She desperately needed an acrylic fill-in. She had already lost three nails.

"I've got a handout that I want you to study, but let's go over a couple of the most important points," Mrs. Smith said, cleaning her hands with a moist napkin. "One, how you present yourself is key, not just the clothes you wear, but your overall presentation during the interview. Dress for success, business attire is the best option. Look the part and you'll be more likely to get it. Two, body language is very important. For instance, shaking hands is a sign of confidence and respect, and so is making regular eye contact with your interviewer. Three, always be polite not just during the interview but to any one you come in contact with in the work environment." Mrs. Smith handed Shaniqua a sheet. "Now, look this over and practice what you want to say."

Shaniqua took the handout, thanked her graciously and left. She glanced over it as she made her way to class, excited that she was another step closer to getting a job.

Over the next couple of weeks, Shaniqua went on a series of interviews, but to no avail. She was growing tired of waiting by the phone. Daily she prayed that someone would want to hire her. She couldn't give up hope. Pastor Cosby had said, "Faith can do things we think are impossible." She had to believe there was a job out there for her somewhere. The following week, Shaniqua was in the kitchen helping Granny cook when she received a phone call requesting a job interview. She was thrilled, but when she learned it was a clothing store for teens, she was ecstatic. Teens Express had all the latest fashions. Brittany and Natasha shopped there, and if she was lucky, she would, too. She needed this job more than any thing. Now all she had to do was convince the manager that she was the best person for the job.

Shaniqua dressed in a knee length, beige dress and matching sling-backs. She gathered her micro braids into a neat low ponytail, smoothed on a light layer of foundation and a dab of lip-gloss. When she finished, she stood in front of the mirror looking as though she was ready for Sunday morning service at church. She quickly snapped on her nameplate necklace to jazz up her outfit. The gold necklace with her name in cursive lettering matched her large earrings, but somehow it didn't look professional. Mrs. Smith's leaflet said to offer the most professional appearance possible. Shaniqua removed both the necklace and earrings, and settled for small hoop earrings. When she made her way downstairs, Granny was stitching a button on her white deaconess blouse in the living room. Her grandmother looked up and smiled. Her mouth offered a small dark hole where her teeth should have been, but they were sitting in a glass jar on the coffee table. "Baby, good luck on yo' interview. You 'member to be polite and use correct grammar." Granny's jaws flapped as she spoke.

Shaniqua giggled. "Yes, ma'am."

"You got bus fare?"

"Yes, ma'am," she said, and left the house.

When Shaniqua arrived at the store, she was directed to a small room in the back. She had been rehearsing what she wanted to say, but she was still nervous, so nervous that she chiseled away the acrylic on a couple of her nails during the bus ride. She couldn't ever recall being this anxious. But she was going to do it. Do it for herself. Do it for Granny. If she was ever going to make something of herself, this was the first step, she thought as she said a silent prayer to God on her way to the back of the store. She was begging for His blessings, pleading with Him to give her the strength to do her best during the interview.

The manager, Cyndi, a thin red-haired woman in her twenties, greeted Shaniqua with a wide, toothy grin. Shaniqua took a seat at a small round table. Cyndi took a few moments to review Shaniqua's application and then smiled. "So, Ms. Williams, tell me something about you."

Shaniqua studied the dusty gray tile and then

remembered that eye contact was essential. When her eyes met Cyndi's, Shaniqua offered a nervous grin. She wasn't sure what to say. "Uh, well, I'm a junior at Miller Grove."

Cyndi nodded. "How are your grades?"

Shaniqua ogled the gray tile once more, stalling to come up with an appropriate answer. She didn't want to tell the woman that she was a below average student, then she would never get the job. "My grades are okay."

Cyndi jotted down something on a yellow steno pad and then looked back to Shaniqua. "Please tell me a strength and a weakness that you possess."

Shaniqua fiddled with her fingers. "One weakness, hmmm, I would have to say time management. I'm not as organized as I should be. But I'm working on it," Shaniqua said, smiling. "And one of my strengths is that I love helping people. Every Sunday at church, my job is to usher the elderly members up the church stairs. I've been doing it since I was ten years old."

Cyndi smiled. "What do you know about our company?"

Shaniqua grinned, relieved to finally have an easy question. "You're a young women's clothing store. I have friends that like to shop here."

Cyndi's smile faded. "Do you know where our corporate office is located?"

A sigh escaped Shaniqua's lips. She had forgotten to do her research on the company. Perspiration beaded on her forehead. She wanted to get up and leave. There was no use in continuing. She had fumbled when it really counted and there was no way she was going to get hired.

Her eyes rested in her lap. "No, ma'am."

"Why should we hire you?"

Shaniqua squirmed in her seat. Her eyes traveled from her lap back to the dusty floor. No words would come. Her thoughts quickly stole back to her life—her mother, her grandmother—their poverty. She couldn't tell a complete stranger that her mother had abandoned her ten years ago and that she recently came back—came back a drug addict, an alcoholic, a thief and God only knew what else. Tears threatened, but she wasn't going to ruin the interview by getting too personal. She had no previous work experience. She held no leadership roles in school. She swallowed hard and spoke slow and deliberately, "Ms. Cyndi, I really need this job. I can do the work. I'm dependable," Shaniqua said. "I live with my grandmother and getting this job would mean the world not only to me, but to my grandmother, too. She needs my help and I really need this job." Shaniqua drew in a deep breath and looked around the room. Boxes were stacked against the wall, a pile of wrinkled cotton shirts were waiting to be steamed. Shaniqua looked back at Cyndi, intensity burning through her eyes. "Ms. Cyndi, if you give me a chance, you will not regret it."

When the interview was over Shaniqua wandered

throughout the mall to relieve stress. She had done her best in the interview, so if she didn't get the job, she wasn't going to worry about it, she told herself. As Mrs. Smith said, "Her interviewing skills would get better the more she did them." She had filled out enough applications and somebody else was bound to call soon. Shaniqua window shopped until temptation was upon her. Cute outfits were everywhere, calling her name. She moseyed into a department store and stumbled on a hot pink and brown shirt on the clearance rack for $13.99. She only had enough money to catch the bus home. She inspected the shirt; there was no alarm on it. She glanced around, there was only one clerk in the juniors department and she was busy at the checkout counter. Shaniqua had to have that shirt. She scanned the area once more to make certain no one was watching. She quickly removed the shirt from the hanger and folded it up tightly. Just as she was about to stuff it into her purse, her mind raced to Pastor Cosby, Mr. Evans, Granny—she quickly changed her mind. She was a new person, maybe not on the outside, but definitely on the inside. She unfolded the shirt, hung it back on the clothes rack and left the mall.

When Shaniqua made it home, Granny was watching TV. "Chile, where you been?"

Shaniqua looked up at the blue-eyed Jesus mounted over the television. "At the mall, I had a job interview, remember?"

"Well, the lady called."

"Really, what did she say?"

"She said you got the job. You can start tomorrow. Be

there at five o'clock. She said call her back if you can't start then."

Shaniqua jumped up and down then ran over to Granny and hugged her tightly. She kissed her sunken cheeks. Her teeth were still soaking in a glass. "I will be there!"

Chapter 25

The next day, Shaniqua sat in English class determined to pay attention. No more pretending to be working but really writing notes to Natasha and Brittany. No more doodling. No more watching lovebirds, Tara and Nicole, pass letters back and forth like their little rainbow clique love affair depended on it. She had made up her mind; she wasn't going to blow school off anymore. When the bell rang, Shaniqua waited for the classroom to empty before she approached the teacher. "Mr. Evans, may I please have a list of my missing assignments?"

Mr. Evans looked up from his desk; a slight smile crept across his face. "Yes, of course. And if you need help, I'm willing to stay after school on Tuesdays and Wednesdays."

"I can come on Wednesdays. On Tuesdays, I go to math tutoring and then, I have to be at work by 5:00 p.m."

Mr. Evans looked impressed. "I know you can do it, Shaniqua. You're every bit as good as anyone else. You just have to believe in you, like I believe in you."

"Yes, sir," Shaniqua said. She didn't want to get him

started again. For some reason, short people loved to climb on soapboxes and announce to the world . . . announce whatever to the world. She hoped she wasn't going to be one of those people when she became successful.

Mr. Evans wrote down the missing assignments. "Now, if you need help, don't hesitate."

Shaniqua grabbed the paper and quickly thanked him. Yes, she had thought about the things that he had said to her, but her newfound motivation was stimulated because of her mother. She would be nothing like Karen. She would be a much better mother to someone some day. She would provide her child with love and money. She would set a good example. Now she knew more than ever that she made the right decision about her pregnancy last year.

After school, Shaniqua hurried through the halls searching for the math tutor room. She had no time to waste. This was going to be the first day on her new job. She thought about skipping tutoring, but she had promised herself—school was going to be a priority from now on. The empty hallways felt eerie. In her three years of going to school there, she had never stayed after, except for cheerleading tryouts, which were a complete waste of time. When she turned the corner, she spotted Stephen and Kendra talking by Kendra's locker. Shaniqua slowed to a turtle's pace. She wished she had a camera phone, but she didn't have a phone at all. She had been asking for a cell phone for Christmas ever since middle school. But Granny made it clear that she didn't have money like that to "waste on foolishness."

Shaniqua inched closer to them, but she couldn't hear. She stretched her neck and strained her ears, but she still couldn't make out what was being said. Suddenly, Stephen flailed his arms. Kendra reached up to hug him. Stephen pushed her back and walked away. Shaniqua waited for him to turn the corner. She moseyed past Kendra trying to see if Kendra was crying, but she couldn't tell because Kendra kept her face inside her locker like she was looking for something. After that stunt Kendra pulled in the lunchroom, Shaniqua wanted to burst out laughing, snap her fingers high in the air and say, "Syke! You ain't takin' my girl's man! Not today girlfriend!" Instead, she kept quiet and continued walking; she didn't have time for the drama. She needed to get to tutoring and then catch the bus to work.

Chapter 26

Shaniqua, Brittany and Natasha were chilling in the commons area like they did most mornings, when Brittany spotted Stephen.

"Tasha, don't look now, but here comes Stephen," Brittany muttered.

"Oh-my-God, Tasha, I forgot to tell you what happened after school yesterday?" Shaniqua said.

Natasha eyes darted back and forth between Brittany and Shaniqua. "What?"

Stephen walked up, looking good in a striped button-down shirt and jeans. "What's up, ladies?"

Everyone spoke but Natasha.

He turned to Natasha, his voice softened as he spoke. "Tasha, you have a minute?"

Natasha turned away from him, "Nope!"

"It's done," Stephen blurted out.

Brittany looked at Shaniqua. "Come on, let's go, girl."

Shaniqua glared at Brittany like she had lost her mind. After a second or two passed, she sighed and then reluctantly said, "See you later, Tasha."

When Brittany and Shaniqua were a good distance away, Stephen started again. “I told Kendra,” he said.

Natasha turned toward Stephen, folding her arms across her chest in defiance. “Oh, really? What did you tell her and why did it take you so long?”

“None of that’s important. Just know that she won’t be hanging around anymore.” Stephen’s voice softened. “Alright, babygirl? I miss you.”

Natasha looked at Stephen, baffled, in love and anger. After a few seconds, a smile crept across her face.

Stephen opened his arms and Natasha went to him. They hugged and kissed, oblivious to their surroundings.

Chapter 27

Brittany missed driving herself to school and to the games. Truth is, she missed her car, even though it wasn't a Lexus. For weeks, her parents chauffeured her around, dropping her off at school and picking her up after cheerleading practice. Finally, Brittany's parents returned her car just in time for her to enjoy the last football game of the season.

When the game ended, Brittany used her cell phone to dial her house. Mr. Brown answered.

"Hi, Daddy, the game's over. We won, finally! Mina, Natasha and Shaniqua would like to get a bite to eat. May I go with them?"

"Where?"

"Stonecrest plaza."

"Be home by eleven o'clock. Now, I would think there is no need for me to go over the consequences . . ."

"No, Dad. I promise I'll be home on time. Thanks, I love you. Bye!" Brittany said, quickly snapped the phone closed before her dad had a chance to ask more questions or worse, change his mind.

Mina staked her claim to the front seat by plopping down.

Shaniqua stared at her, slapping her with her eyeballs. "Oh, no, she didn't. Who told her she could sit in the front seat?"

Mina turned to face Shaniqua sitting in the back. "Is there a problem?"

"Yeah, you . . ."

Natasha jabbed Shaniqua in the leg to be quiet.

Brittany got in and cranked up the radio. "So where do you guys want to eat?"

Mina shouted, "Let's do 'Five Guys!'"

Everyone laughed.

Brittany turned into the parking lot of the restaurant, scanning the vehicles for Marcus's hooptie of a truck. She knew how much he liked their cheeseburgers and Cajun fries. She was relieved when she didn't see his Blazer. Brittany glanced at Mina. "Where's Carlos hanging out tonight?"

Mina huffed. "No where. He said he had a lot of projects due or something."

Brittany sneered. "Carlos does homework?"

Shaniqua leaned forward. "Uh, y'all guess what? I got an eighty-seven on my math test today!"

Natasha high-fived Shaniqua. "You go, girl!"

Brittany looked at Shaniqua through her rear-view mirror, "Shaniqua, I had that math class my freshman year. Needless to say, I got an A."

Natasha spoke up, "You are right, it is needless to say. Can't we ever talk about somebody other than Brittany Brown?"

Brittany smirked. "Yes, you can, but then the conversation would be quite bor . . . ing!"

"There is no hope for you!" Shaniqua said.

The girls entered the restaurant and claimed a table near the front. The restaurant was packed and noisy, everything from high-pitched squeals to low masculine chuckles. Most kids were in groups, talking, eating, and poking fun at other students. Brittany was ecstatic to be hanging out with everyone and not feeling guilty about doing it. Her parents knew exactly where she was. She had worked hard over the past few weeks to gain their trust now it was time to show and prove. She was going to make sure she made it home ahead of time, at least ten minutes early. Suddenly Brittany heard a female voice squeal, "Marcus!" She looked to Mina. Mina heard it, too. They both glanced around the restaurant. Both of them were equally surprised. Marcus was tickling some girl, while Carlos had his arm around a cheerleader from his school.

Mina was sitting in the seat closest to the wall; Brittany was seated on the end. "Oh, hell no," Mina said, trying to move Brittany out of the way. "Let me out!"

Shaniqua glared at Brittany. "Let her out!" Then Shaniqua stood up and escorted Mina out. "I'll go with you."

Natasha shook her head. "Shaniqua ain't big as a baby ant, what does she think she's going to do?"

Brittany shrugged her shoulders. "Well, I'm not going over there because I don't want Marcus to think that I give a rat's tail about his new girlfriend."

Mina and Shaniqua made it to Carlos and Marcus's table. Mina planted her hands on her hips. "Carlos, what are you doing?"

Carlos took his arm from around the girl. "What does it look like . . . eating."

Mina nodded. "Oh, it's like that, now, huh!"

Carlos turned his attention back to the girl sitting beside him.

Tears mounted in Mina's eyes as she started back to her table. "Te odio! Cadron!"

The girls quickly paid their bill and left. Once in the car, everyone was talking except Mina. She was sniffling and muttering, "I can't believe he did that to me! I hate him! He is so stupid!"

"Well, you didn't need his sorry ass anyway putting his hands on you," Shaniqua blurted out.

The car fell silent while the engine purred.

Brittany frowned. "Shaniqua, shut up!"

"Why I got to shut up? You and Tasha always frontin'. Don't act like we ain't all been talkin' 'bout Mina gettin' her head tagged."

Brittany swallowed hard; she knew her eyes had to be bugged out of her head. She had promised Mina that she wouldn't tell anyone.

Silence loomed.

Brittany turned to face Mina, but got only her profile. Brittany lifted her right hand off the steering wheel in an effort to console Mina, but put it back. After a few seconds, Brittany found her voice. "I'm sorry. I was just concerned about you so I asked Natasha if she knew of something that you could do to protect yourself from him."

Mina said nothing. The silence was so complete that they could hear the unevenness of her breathing.

Natasha fiddled with her fingers trying to decide if she should speak up. "Mina, we just met and I don't know you very well, but one thing my dad has always told me, 'If a boy puts his hands on you, that means he doesn't love you or care about you.' He says, 'Boys will do that when they have low self-esteem or when they feel powerless.' My dad's a DeKalb County police officer if you want to come over my house to talk with him."

An expression of pain and inward concentration altered the pale contours of Mina's face. "I don't need to talk to a cop."

Natasha leaned forward in the seat. "No, I'm just saying he'll tell you all the legal things that you can do if Carlos puts his hands on you again."

Mina turned around and faced the group. "Did you

guys not see Carlos in the restaurant with another girl? I'm through with him. We've been together since my freshman year, and now I'm through with him. I'm not going through this again. He's so stupid!"

No one was certain which part of it Mina was through with, the violence or the cheating, so everyone remained quiet. Brittany turned up the radio. The hum of the car, coupled with the music, eased the awkward silence as Brittany dropped her friends off at their homes.

When Brittany finally made it home, it was ten forty-five. Her dad was in the kitchen eating a bowl of ice cream with strawberry flavoring drizzled on top. "You're early, how was everything?" Mr. Brown said.

"Good. We had fun. Thanks for trusting me, Daddy."

"No problem, princess, you've earned it. Over the past few weeks, you've called when you said you would. You were home by curfew, so you deserved to have your driving privileges reinstated. All we wanted you to do was get to a point where we could feel comfortable letting you go, knowing that you're going to return on time. You're maturing."

"You think?" she said, sarcastically. She hadn't changed, they had, but she wasn't about to argue her point. It was useless to battle with them. "Daddy, can I please change my hideous-looking bedroom? I feel like sleeping beauty in there. I want something more contemporary. My bedroom should reflect me."

"What do you have in mind?"

Brittany shrugged. "I don't know. How about leopard print?"

Mr. Brown offered a curious look.

She chuckled. "Okay, maybe not leopard print, but I'll start looking. Okay?"

"Alright, princess. Now, give your daddy a kiss."

Brittany eased over to her dad. "Dad, I'm really too old for this."

Mr. Brown spun around. "Oh yeah, you think so... huh," and tickled Brittany until she cried out, "Okay, okay! I give!"

Chapter 28

Brittany and Natasha stood inside the mall watching Shaniqua through the glass window. She was busy hanging clothes on a rack in the back and laughing with the manager. Brittany and Natasha let out mischievous giggles as they tiptoed into the store, trying to sneak up on Shaniqua. They made their way back to the t-shirt rack. Natasha grabbed a white Urban Goddess tee and stuck it halfway in her purse. Brittany giggled, then grabbed a black Ms. Thang tee and stuffed it inside her jacket. Natasha fought to keep a straight face.

Shaniqua turned around and caught Brittany in the act. She cleared her throat to get her friend's attention without alerting her boss. They pretended not to hear, then slowly made their way to the front of the store. Fear gripped Shaniqua, rendering her motionless and speechless. She stood frozen like a deer trapped in the trance of headlights. A pair of jeans draped her shoulders. Sweat beaded on her forehead. She couldn't believe her friends were doing this to her. This was the best thing that ever happened to her, now her friends were going to ruin it. Why were they doing this to her? Tears threatened. Shaniqua peeked at her manager still busy steaming a new shipment of cotton shirts. Her manager had no clue to the catastrophe that loomed in the air with the loud music. Shaniqua made angry eyes at them, and shook her head to prevent them from walking out of the store.

They were just a couple of feet from the entrance when Natasha whispered, "One, two, three." Brittany and Natasha spun around and yelled in unison, "Got cha' back!"

Everyone in the store looked at them. Shaniqua let out a nervous laugh and looked to her boss who was wearing a curious smile. Brittany and Natasha made their way to the cash register. Shaniqua met them there. She paused for a moment and mopped her brow.
"Uh, I swear to God, well, not to God, but I'm going to get y'all, y'all are wrong for that!"

Brittany and Natasha laughed until their stomachs ached.

Chapter 29

Shaniqua couldn't ever remember being so excited to get her report card, except maybe in fourth grade when she had gotten all B's and one A. But that was before school had become difficult. Her heart pounded as her homeroom teacher, Mrs. Roberson, called students up to her desk to receive their white envelope. She wondered if her efforts would indeed pay off. All of her free time was spent either working at the clothing store or at tutoring. She had put in extra work trying to learn everything that she had missed over the past couple of years. Secretly, she always doubted that she had the ability to learn and now that she actually took the time to apply herself, the results were in. Her fingers trembled as she opened the envelope. She pulled out the blue and white sheet of paper. She scrolled down the page, class by class. Every score on the paper was an 80 and above. Happy tears filled her eyes. She was elated that she had gotten all B's and C's. She glanced around the classroom and dried her eyes quickly. She was so proud of herself; she wanted to shout it to everyone in the class that she wasn't a dummy after all. She could achieve good grades, too. She couldn't wait to share the news with Granny, but first she had to tell her girls.

Shaniqua sat at the cafeteria table waiting, scanning the area for Brittany and Natasha. She could hardly contain her excitement when she saw them. "Where's Mina?"

Brittany sat her lunch tray down and shrugged. "She's still not talking to me."

"Hello, somebody!" Shaniqua struck a sassy pose. "Holla at a goddess!"

Brittany and Natasha looked at one another and then stared at Shaniqua like she was crazy.

Shaniqua beamed a wide smile. "I got all B's and C's!"

Natasha got up and ran around the table. "Give me a hug! Girl, you did your thang."

Brittany stood up, too. "Yeah, girl," she said, slapping Shaniqua high five from across the table. "Now, let's see who can get the best grades by the end of the school year."

Natasha sneered. "Is that really necessary? Why are you always trying to compete?"

Shaniqua interjected, "No, Tasha. It's cool!"

"Okay, here's the deal, we each put in one hundred dollars in the pot and at the end of the year, whoever has the highest grades wins the money," Brittany said.

Shaniqua nodded. "Cool, Ms. Thang. Hang if you can hang!"

Brittany stuck out her pinky finger. "Pinky promise."

Natasha smirked. "Uh, Brittany, we're not in kindergarten!"

They all laughed!

Other books by Sonia Hayes from the ATL Girlz series:

Book I
Ms. Thang
ISBN 978-0-9777573-0-5

Book II
Urban Goddess
ISBN 978-0-9777573-1-2

Book III
Eye Candy
ISBN 978-0-9777573-2-9

T-Shirt Giveaway

One lucky reader will be selected every month to receive a free T-shirt.

❑ Ms. Thang fitted T-shirt
Size: ❑ S ❑ M ❑ L ❑ XL

❑ Urban Goddess fitted T-shirt
Size: ❑ S ❑ M ❑ L ❑ XL

Please submit this page to enter. Duplicate entries or photocopies will not be accepted. Please print legibly. You will be notified via e-mail.

Name:______________________________________

Address:____________________________________

City __________________State_____Zip_______-___

Email:______________________________________

<u>Please Mail to:</u>
NUA Multimedia
4611 Hardscrabble Road
Suite 109, PMB 309
Columbia, SC 29229

GOOD LUCK!

Q U I C K   O R D E R   F O R M

Have your credit card ready.

Fax order:	803.419.8787. *(Send this form.)*
Telephone order:	803.246.5547.
E-mail order:	orders@soniahayes.com
Postal order:	NUA Multimedia 4611 Hardscrabble Road, Suite 109 PMB 309 Columbia, SC 29229. USA

Please send the following:

❑ Ms. Thang Novel ($9.95 ea.)

❑ Urban Goddess Novel ($9.95 ea.)

❑ Ms. Thang fitted T-shirt – Size S, M, L, XL ($14.95 ea.)

❑ Urban Goddess fitted T-shirt – Size S, M, L, XL ($14.95 ea.)

Special Offer ~ Buy one book and one shirt for $20.00

Please mail to:

Name:____

Address:______________________________________

City __________________State____Zip_________-_____

Telephone: ____________________________________

Email: _______________________________________

Shipping by air:

❑ US: $4 for the first product and $2 for each additional product.

❑ International: $9 for the first product and $5 for each additional product. (estimate)

Payment: ❑ Money Order ❑ Check ❑ Credit card:
❑ Visa ❑ MasterCard ❑ AMEX ❑ Discover

Card number ___________________________________

Name on card _____________________Exp. Date________

Signature _____________________________________

Believe in You!